The Per[...]

By Haylee Reid and Her Classmates

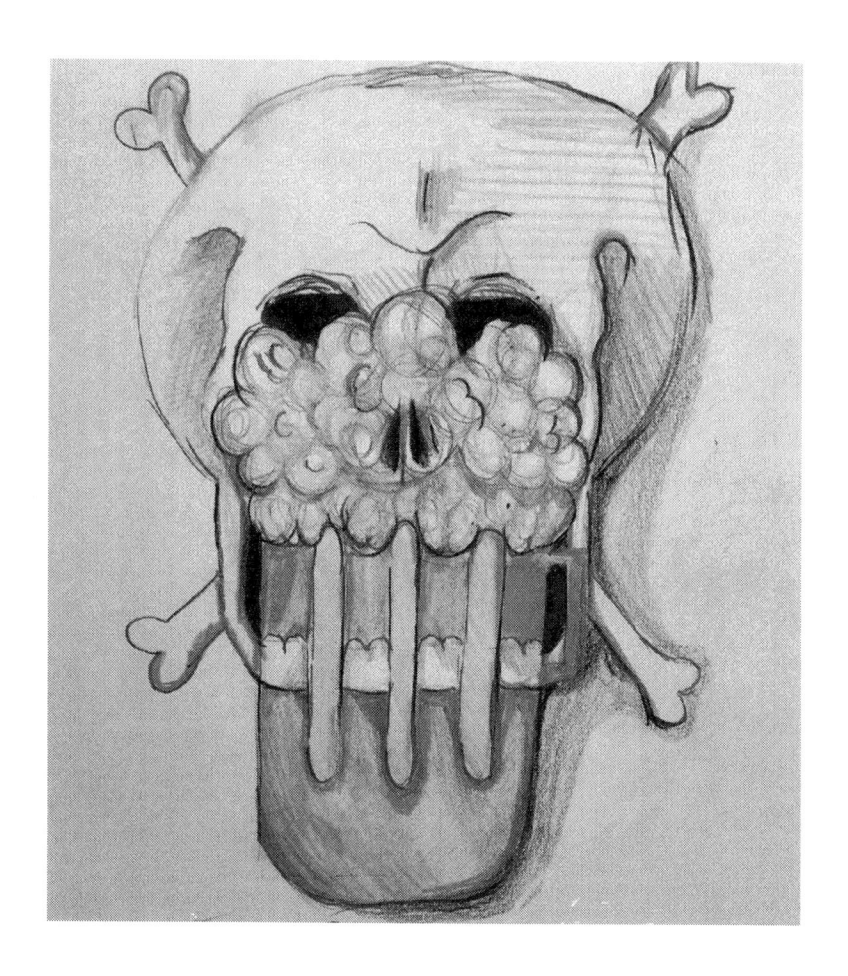

The Perfect Couple and Other Stories

Copyright © 2024 by Deep Read Press

All Rights Reserved.

The publisher prohibits the reproduction, scanning, or distribution of this book in any printed or electronic form without permission, except for brief passages quoted as part of a literary review.

Please do not take part in or encourage piracy of copyrighted materials in violation of the author's rights. Purchase only authorized editions.

The publisher does not control and does not assume any responsibility for the author's or any third-party websites or their content. Views expressed here are the author's alone.

First Deep Read Press Edition.

Published in the United States of America

Edited by: Brenda LeCrone Seaberg

Cover Design by: Kim Gammon

Cover Image by: Harlow Willbanks

Title Page Image by: Libby Sircy

Paperback ISBN: 978-1-954989-55-9

Published by:
DEEP READ PRESS
Lafayette, Tennessee
www.deepreadpress.com
deepreadpress@gmail.com

Contents

Introduction – p. 4

1. The Perfect Couple – p. 5
2. The Seven Trumpets – p. 13
3. The Run – p. 17
4. What Lies Beyond the Field – p. 24
5. A Thin Line Between Love and Death – p. 30
6. Smokey Mountain Mystery – p. 41
7. The Loop – p. 48
8. I Thank God – p. 55
9. Sleepover Gone Wrong – p. 60
10. Schizophrenia: The Cycle – p. 66
11. Gut Feeling – p. 73
12. Barbed Wire – p. 80

Introduction

It is an understatement to say that I am proud of the students who wrote the stories that make up this collection. They formulated their own ideas, wrote various drafts of their stories, proofread each other's work, and incorporated feedback from their peers and teacher in revising their writing. Throughout the process, they learned a great deal about being creative, developing their ideas, evaluating others' work, giving and receiving thoughtful feedback, and collaborating with fellow students. While I am confident that the experience of publishing this book was meaningful to each participant, I am hopeful that reading it will bring you much pleasure.

Deric McClard

1. The Perfect Couple
By Haylee Reid

Everything in their relationship was perfect at first. Neither of them had been disloyal, or anything even close to it. In fact, August never talked to other guys once she had gotten together with Holden. They were the longest-lasting couple in the whole school.

Holden was a good boyfriend. Many girls wanted to be with him and were jealous of August. She knew this and found it funny how girls could hate her just because she was dating the boy they wanted.

August was an amazing girlfriend. They had started dating at the beginning of her freshman year, which was Holden's sophomore year. Holden had shown some jealous tendencies. He would get mad if she even came in contact with another guy. August thought it was normal, though.

He would occasionally drink sometimes, too. Even though drinking was illegal at his age, his parents never cared. He would get the alcohol from his older cousin, and often, they would drink together. August never allowed him to be around her while he was drunk. But that was what people saw from the outside looking in.

Holden called August around 7:00 pm, just like he had been doing for the past year. They usually fell asleep on the phone.

"Hey, where are you?" Holden asked. He could hear that she was in a car, and he heard a group of girls screaming and laughing.

"I'm riding around with my friends!"

There was music blasting and girls yelling. He could barely hear August, so he just hung up. He already had a headache, and he didn't like it when she was with her friends. She usually got home late, and she wouldn't talk to him much. And all her friends were single. They talked to guys everywhere they went, but August always swore she was never a part of that. Holden believed her, but still worried about the guys she could be talking to.

There was a ding from his phone, so he picked it up and read the text: *Are you seriously mad at me right now?* He chose to ignore it because he didn't want to argue.

There was another ding: *You always do this. You're so immature.*

He knew she didn't mean it. She always said things she didn't mean when she got upset. He replied: *Talk later.* Then, he set his phone down and fell asleep.

At 11:23 p.m., she finally texted him again: *Hey, I'm home. You haven't been active, so I'm guessing you're sleeping.*

He woke up to the sounds of the dings, and immediately texted back: *I was asleep. I'm sorry about earlier. I wasn't mad. My head just hurt, and I was tired.*

She called him, and he answered, laying his phone on his bed: *I'm going back to sleep. Goodnight.*

She laughed: *No, you're not. You're staying up and talking to me. It's a Friday night, and it's only 11:30.*

Where were you? he asked.

We went to eat Mexican food. Then, we went to Target and messed around for a while. But I started missing you, so I came home.

He smiled a little and nodded as though she could see him.

She started telling him what they did at Target, but he fell asleep within two minutes.

The next morning, August got up and got ready. Holden was coming to the mall with her and her family. She took a shower, ate breakfast, then brushed her teeth.

He came over after she got ready. They hung out a little and then made their way to the mall. They spent the whole day together and had so much fun. But that night, Holden called August. He told her they needed to talk about their relationship. He sounded really upset, and it worried her. "What about our relationship?" August said.

"I just don't think that we are going to work out. I'm sorry."

August didn't know what to say. Her mouth gaped, and she stared at the wall in front of her.

"Oh. Why?"

"Well, you're always with your friends. We used to hang out all the time, and now it's all about your friends. That's not the only reason, though."

"What are the other reasons?" Her voice broke, and she started to feel tears in her eyes.

"I'm just not happy anymore. It's not the same. I still love you, just not romantically."

She went silent again, and the next thing she heard was the sound of the end of the call.

She slammed the phone down, getting angry instead of sad. They had been together for so long, and he wanted to break up because she hung out with her friends?

"Whatever," she muttered, then left the house. She walked down the street to her best friend's house. She cried, and they watched movies and ate ice cream for the rest of the night.

About two weeks later, her best friend set her up with a guy. She started talking to him, and they hit it off almost immediately.

About a month later, August had been talking to the guy she got set up with. Her ex, Holden, hadn't moved on at all. She had been seeing him around the school in random, unusual places. She found it weird, but never thought too much of it.

August and her new guy, Noah, had been out on a few dates. Occasionally, she had seen her ex. She shrugged it off because she felt safe with Noah.

Noah was a better guy than Holden. Holden knew this, and that's why he was so angry she was with him now. Noah didn't talk to other girls, and he was all about August. They hadn't had a single fight yet, and he didn't mind when she hung out with her friends. He was everything August wanted.

"I have a way better feeling about Noah than I ever did about Holden," August's mom said. "I always knew you could do better than Holden. Both in personality and looks." August laughed at that, and was happy to realize that she didn't miss him at all anymore.

That Friday night, Noah was planning to go over to August's house. They had planned to eat dinner and watch a movie, and then he would leave around 11:00 or 12:00 that night. August's mom was pretty relaxed with Noah, but she would never allow sleepovers.

August came home from school, setting her phone down on the counter and telling her mom about her day. Suddenly, her phone started ringing. She picked it up, expecting to see a number. Instead of a number, she saw "No Caller ID." She figured it was spam and declined the call. Then, she got another call. "No Caller ID." She declined once again, but her phone didn't stop ringing. She got frustrated, set her phone down, and walked away to help her mom clean the living room.

She went back to her phone after about twenty minutes, and there were almost ninety missed calls from "No Caller ID." She thought it was someone trying to play a prank or something. She shrugged it off and went into her room, getting ready for Noah to come over.

Noah arrived a little after her dad had gotten home. Her mom and dad started to make dinner while Noah and August went down to the basement. August turned on her favorite movie, and they waited for the food to get done. Shortly after turning the movie on, Noah turned to August.

"I think it's time that I tell you how I really feel." Noah's tone was off, and it scared August. She thought he was about to break things off between them, and that's not what she wanted at all. "I love you," he said instead. August was shocked. She didn't expect to hear those words come from him. She didn't know what to say because she wasn't sure that she truly loved him yet.

August's mother called them up for dinner, which gave August time to think of what to say. They ate dinner, talked, and laughed with each other. It was never awkward with Noah and her parents, and she was happy about that.

After dinner, Noah and August went to her room. Her parents' rule was that they had to keep the door open, which was perfectly fine with them. Noah looked at August, wanting to continue the conversation from earlier. August looked at him awkwardly. "I didn't really expect this, so I'm a little confused about what to say," she said.

He looked a little hurt at her words. "Just tell me how you feel," he urged.

She nodded, "Then I guess I should tell you I—"

August was cut off by the sound of a rock hitting the window. She jumped, and so did Noah. They both looked at each other and then back at the window, which now had a little crack, and August got scared.

Noah went over to the window and looked outside to see who was there. He didn't see anyone, so he turned back to August and shrugged. "I didn't see anybody. I don't know who threw the rock."

August nodded, thinking it was some of the neighborhood boys playing a prank. Then, August thought back to all the "No Caller ID" calls she had gotten earlier that day. She started to get worried and thought about the possibility of having a stalker.

She sat on her bed, Noah sitting beside her. "I'm sure it was nothing to be worried about," Noah said reassuringly. August nodded, even though Noah didn't look so sure about what he had just said.

Suddenly, another rock hit the window, fully breaking it. The sound was loud. August's parents had been asleep for almost thirty minutes, and she was surprised it didn't wake them up. Noah started to get up, but August grabbed his arm and shook her head.

"Don't go anywhere. Someone's out there, and they might be dangerous." Then they heard the front door creak open. Noah and August looked at each other, and both of them had a scared expression. There was the loud sound of someone stomping through the house.

August screamed and looked towards the door to see who it was. Holden was standing there, a mix of hurt and anger on his face. She could smell the scent of alcohol coming from his clothes.

"How could you do this to me, August?"

Both August and Noah were in disbelief.

"Do what?" Noah asked suspiciously.

Holden looked at Noah and got even angrier. "Move on!? It's only been a month! How could you move on so fast?"

August's mouth fell open. "You were the one who broke up with me! I found Noah and realized he was willing to treat me right! Why would I pass that up?"

Holden stared at her for a moment. He didn't know what to say. "Okay, you know what? Break it off with him and get back with me. Right now," he finally said.

August looked at him in disbelief. "I'm not breaking it off with Noah. I see a future with him. He's treated me better in a month than you ever have!"

All of a sudden, Holden pulled a gun from his waistband. August screamed and backed up to the wall. Holden yelled, "Break it off with him now!"

Noah was trying to come up with something to do, and August started crying. Noah looked at August. "Just break it off. That's better than one of us getting hurt, August."

Noah acted like he didn't care, so she could tell it was some kind of plan. "Fine. I'm done."

Noah nodded, looking down at the floor. Holden smirked, putting the gun down. "Now, August, come with me. We are leaving so we can talk this out."

August stayed silent and walked towards Holden. Noah knew August had a metal softball bat under her bed, so Noah grabbed the bat. He swung it at Holden, hitting him on the head and knocking him down. Holden yelled and held his head. Noah got on top of him, then grabbed the gun from Holden's hand.

"GET OUT OF HERE!" Noah screamed at Holden. It scared August because she had never seen him mad before. Especially this mad. Noah held the gun and grabbed Holden's arm. Noah pulled him up, shoving him. "GO!"

Holden was still in shock as he walked out the door, got in his truck, and drove away. August was still crying, so Noah comforted her until she was okay. Afterwards, he made a bed on the floor, not wanting to leave the house in case Holden came back. August fell asleep, but Noah stayed up half the night.

The next day, Noah and August explained everything to her parents. Her parents were going to press charges and get a restraining order. What Holden did was unforgivable.

They took him to court and got the restraining order. Both August and Noah got one since he had threatened them both.

Six years later, August and Noah got married. Later on, they had kids. Neither of them had heard from Holden since that night, but they had heard that he was always drunk and almost never went out of his house.

He never dated anyone again because he thought that August was the one for him. He thought she would eventually come back to him, so he waited for her. She never went back, and he died from liver failure.

2. The Seven Trumpets
By Parker Hewitt

I never thought it would happen this soon. I thought I would live a successful life without having to worry about anything. I always considered myself a religious man, but I never gave thought to when the end events in the Bible would actually happen.

    That was before the great fire. I was studying in my dorm room when it happened. I looked outside, and to my horror, half the campus was ablaze with fire raging for miles. I gathered my belongings and ran out of my dorm. I ran to my car and pulled out of the charred campus. As I was driving, I called my parents for help. They told me I could stay at their beach house near the ocean because it wasn't far from my campus. About half an hour later, I arrived at the house.

I unpacked what I had been able to grab from my dorm. The rest was probably charred. It had been years since I'd been to the house, so I had to get my bearings. After looking around, I decided to sit down and watch some television to get my mind off things. As I watched, I saw that a meteor was heading towards the Pacific Ocean, the ocean where I was conveniently staying. While I was getting my bearings a moment earlier, I had seen a basement full of canned vegetables. I quickly brought my computer and some other essentials down there. I tensed up in the cellar, waiting for it to come. I got on my computer and searched for information about the meteor. It had just hit, and it caused a tsunami that was heading my way. I heard the crack of the building above me. The meteor had caused a tsunami, but somehow the basement door let no water in. The shelves, because of the massive crash above me, fell over. One of the glass jars fell on my head, and I was out cold.

When I woke up, I heard the sound of a helicopter and saw two men lifting the shelves off me. They gave me medication and told me I was going somewhere safe. I dozed off in the helicopter and woke up on a bed. I saw lots of people in other beds around me. A doctor came over and informed me that I had nearly been killed by internal bleeding. Luckily, the Coast Guard had been able to save me before any more damage was done. They had transported me to a forest region in Missouri.

They hadn't been so lucky with others. Thousands had been killed. I tried to get up, shocked at this news, but slowly lay back down due to the pain my effort caused me. I had to rest for a couple of days before I was able to get up without much pain. I was very thirsty, but they couldn't give me any water; they had to save it. They said all the natural reserves were dirty. The ocean was also way too dirty to purify. The unclean water alone killed many people. Since water at the facility was running low, I was asked to go out and try to find some clean water.

As I was walking in the forest, I found a spring. However, as I bent down to drink from it, it started to turn brown. In shock, I fell back and looked up. A giant object hit the sun. As it hit, the entire world darkened. Most of the sun flew off into space, but parts of it fell to earth. They destroyed parts of the forest and set fire to the rest around me.

I ran as fast as I could back to the camp. As I got to a cliff overlooking the camp, I saw hundreds of people destroying the camp and hurting each other. As I saw this, I felt rage enter into me. I climbed down from the cliff and lunged at as many people as I saw. I would hit someone and then get hit by someone else. I must've gotten hit hundreds of times. Each hit hurt worse than the one before it, but I wasn't dying. I saw that even though people were mauling each other, they never failed to loot each other's pockets. Suddenly, I heard a noise beside me. There must have been millions of bugs. Locusts, I believe. Without warning, they suddenly started biting me and the others around me. I ran as fast as I could.

The locusts covered the sky. It was nearly pitch black. I saw lights in the distance and ran towards them. I ran for what seemed like hours. My sense of time was destroyed by the fact that I was being stung thousands of times. As I got to the light, I tripped. I fell on top of a pile of bodies. I was surrounded by a burning city. I saw hundreds of people running. About a third of the number of people running were dead. There were still people being hit and robbed all around me. Evil seemed to prevail.

As I stood there, I heard a mighty sound. It was thunder. But it didn't sound once; it sounded seven times consecutively. The thunder sounded like words. They spoke loudly: "There will be no more delay!" Then, there was a beautiful light, so beautiful that it hurt my eyes to look at it. It burned my skin. Someone from the light descended in front of me. It was the face of Jesus Christ. He said that what I had just seen with my own eyes was soon to come. He told me to get right with Him. Then, he said, "Depart from me, for I don't know you!"

Suddenly, I woke up. That couldn't have been a dream. It was way too realistic. I lifted my head off of my books and looked outside. No fire. No bodies. Everything was normal. I quickly got up and ran to my bookcase. I scrambled around until I found a book that read *Holy Bible*. I turned to the Book of Revelation and saw that what I had dreamed is said one day to happen. Prophecy soon to be fulfilled. What I saw wasn't a coincidence. It was a sign. A sign to leave my old life behind and have a new life in Jesus.

3. The Run

By Annalise Brooks and Madelyne Winfree

I love going on morning walks. Yes, I know, it's a very unpopular opinion, but I love them. I have a short trail I walk on that loops around a graveyard that I deem haunted and that is owned by someone whom I don't know. I've always loved walking in the fall, especially because when I go on my walks, like now, the morning breeze just makes everything feel right. And trust me, there's a lot wrong with my life. I am a 16-year-old girl in a messed-up world.

To start off, my father is an avaricious workaholic who ropes my mother into all of his business affairs. My parents make it seem like everything they do is completely normal, but I know that deep down it's not. We don't go on family vacations, and I don't get to go to summer camps, or do any of the things that normal 16-year-olds do. I'm homeschooled because my parents say they are "worried for my safety," but I know it's really because they don't want me to be seen. They don't know that I know this, but a few days ago, I found out everything. As I pass my house, still running, I hear my mother's voice echo from the porch, telling me I have a phone call. I dart inside, eager to see who is calling me.

"Hello?" I say into the phone.

"Hey, Pumpkin!" the gruff voice says enthusiastically. I breathe a sigh of relief as I recognize my uncle's voice. I don't mind his company, since he is the only family member who actually treats me like the 16-year-old I am. I feel as though he understands me in some different way.

After I reply to the greeting, I roll my eyes at the nickname I was given when I was 7. It was Thanksgiving, and I had really enjoyed the pumpkin pie. It had ended up all over my face, and this gave everyone a good laugh. It was one of the last times I remember being happy. I quickly came back to the present, having forgotten he was still on the phone.

"What's up?" I say, a little suspiciously. He doesn't call much, but when he does, he doesn't normally sound this cheery. But I'm happy, nonetheless.

"So, I have great news. I'm coming down to visit on Monday!"

I pause for a moment before responding because it has been so long since he last visited. We've had phone calls, but not any visits since he lives in another state.

"Really? Is everything okay?"

"Yeah, everything is, uh…fine, yeah."

I knew by the way he said that, everything is not fine. My parents and friends have a habit of saying things that obviously aren't true, for to them, I am just a little girl who doesn't know right or wrong. So, of course, they put no effort into trying to make their words believable. But I am definitely more observant than anyone gives me credit for.

After a beat, I ask, "So, how long are you staying?" knowing he would soon have to get off the phone.

"About three weeks. Maybe longer. It just depends on..." he pauses for a moment, searching for the right word, "business."

"Of course, business," I add, skeptically. I can almost feel him staring at me, the way he does when he can tell I'm questioning something through the phone.

After a pause that seems to last forever, he eventually says, "Ok, well, I have to go. I'll see you soon, Pumpkin." The call ends. Something is wrong, I can tell. I just can't fully grasp what it is yet.

"Who was on the phone, Sweetie?"

I quickly snap out of my daze. "It was Unc–" Before I can finish the sentence, something in me says not to tell her who it was. I don't know why, but it's almost as if she knows what's going on, and if she knows he's coming for a visit, she'll never let me get to the bottom of this. "Oh, nobody. You don't really know him," I say. I have always been good at lying.

"Oh...ok," she says. I thought I had made it seem believable, but from the tone of her voice, I'm not so sure.

"I'm gonna head up to my room. I have some schoolwork I need to catch up on," I say, tugging on my necklace. I just want to get out of there so I can think about the phone call. There's obviously something going on with Uncle Rob, and I have to figure out what.

"Ok, Love, don't forget about your English test Friday. Make sure to study for that, too," she says, as a warm smile spreads across her face.

"I will, don't worry." Before she can say anything else, I'm already racing up the stairs.

I basically hide out in my room until my uncle arrives. I am so excited, the two days it takes feel like centuries. Finally, I hear a sharp knock on the door. I practically leap over all the stairs and swing open the door.

"There's my favorite girl!" He looks exactly the same. I haven't seen him in a long time, so I expect him to have aged a little, but he hasn't at all. He still has on that same red scarf he always wears. It makes me smile a little. I jump into his open arms and hug him tightly. I'm beyond glad that someone whom I can actually relate to is in the house.

"I've missed you so much!!" I exclaim, as he sets me back down on the ground.

"You, too, Pumpkin."

"Wow! You've grown up so much since the last time I saw you," he says. I incline my head slightly and glance away.

He's always complained about me growing up too fast, but now it seems as though he is proud of how far I've come. That thought makes me smile to myself.

"I'm so glad you're here! I'll go get Mom. You can wait in the living room!" I can barely contain my excitement.

After I get my mom, we talk for hours before I finally go to bed. As I fall asleep, I think about asking him to go on my run with me, but decide against it. He's probably tired, and besides, it's my thing. I don't want to share it with anyone, no matter who it is.

~~~~~~~~~
12:00 AM
~~~~~~~~~

I wake up abruptly to sounds of yelling coming from across the hall. My father's office. That means fighting, which means my father is mad at my uncle again. I quietly plant my feet on the cold floor and creep to the entrance of the office to listen through the door.

"I TOLD YOU I NEEDED THE MONEY BY DECEMBER!" my uncle shouts.

"IT'S OCTOBER!!" my dad shouts back. I know it's bad if my uncle is raising his voice. He hardly ever yells at anyone. When he does, you know someone has made him really mad.

"DECEMBER OF 2022," my uncle shrills. I stand there, trying to recall what would make Uncle Rob ask for money. In the past, he and my dad weren't overly friendly, but they were at least civil with each other.

"You have always been just so greedy. I don't even blame Dad for despising you," my father spits out.

My uncle's face turns even more red. He looks terrifying. He takes a short, ragged breath. "You're going to wish you'd never said that," he replies angrily. As their volume rises, so does my heart rate. I look away for two seconds, and when I turn back, my uncle is on the ground with a bloody nose.

"Dad...? Uncle Rob?" I ask. I'm used to being around conflict at my house, but hardly ever like this. They sound like they want to kill each other. My dad shoots Uncle Rob a dirty look.

"Look what you did, you buffoon! You woke up my daughter!" My dad isn't yelling as loudly now, but his expression is unchanging. "I want you out of my house," he demands.

My uncle, still lying on the ground, doesn't move.

"NOW!" my father roars. Uncle Rob stands up and swiftly walks out of the room. I stand frozen in place, in shock. I have never seen my father and uncle fight like this.

"Sweetie! Let me explain!" my dad pleads, but it's too late, I am already on my way downstairs. I have to find Uncle Rob.

When I see him, he's lying on the couch with a bag of frozen peas on his face.

"Hey, Pumpkin," he says. He's barely conscious. I'm not surprised because I know how strong my father is.

"What was that? My dad totally just knocked you out for no reason!" I exclaim.

"It's nothing. Your father just owes me a little money, and I know how to get it. Go back to sleep," he says. I then turn around to grab a Band-Aid for the cut on his lip. I reach up to the cabinet and grab the first-aid kit. I unwrap one and turn to hand it to him. When I do, there's a cold, indiscernible look on his face that I've never seen before. It's as if he has completely desensitized himself to everything and everyone. I fix my confused stare on his face a little longer before I go back to my room without another word.

~~~~~~~~~

4:00 AM

~~~~~~~~~

I can't sleep. I haven't slept since I saw my father hit my uncle. I can't forget the way his face looked when he told me what had happened. What did he mean by "I know how to get it?" I sit and stare up at the ceiling. Something is wrong. My stomach is in knots. I feel like I need to know what's going on, so I creep back to my father's office. I look in every drawer, through every cabinet, on every shelf, for something that would hint at why they were fighting like that, when, all of a sudden, I find it. I am looking through one of the last drawers when I see stacks and stacks of papers. That is weird in itself, since my father keeps everything in our house extremely organized, so to see that many papers just scattered around in a drawer is very odd. As I start looking through them, I realize what they are. Hundreds of bills that are supposed to be paid by my father to my uncle, dating back as far as three years ago. My father is in debt. To his brother. That's what it is. I'm in complete and utter shock. He owes my uncle hundreds of dollars, maybe thousands. I sneak back to my room to think about what I had seen. I have no idea what to do. Because I still can't sleep, I decide to take my morning walk early. It's VERY early, but I have nothing better to do. I put on some leggings and a long-sleeve shirt, grab my coat, and sneak out the door. I just start walking. After an indeterminate amount of time, as I start to go to the graveyard, I feel two hands grab my waist and pull me backwards.

"Don't. Say. A. Word." My instincts kick in too late, but I try to turn around. I get a flash of red clothing before the person yanks me back.

"Who ar–" I'm cut off by the sharp clap of a hand on my mouth. I have no idea who this person is or what he or she wants.

Before I can even begin to think about who it could be, the person picks me up and throws me across his or her shoulder. A man. That's the one thing I know for sure. No woman could pick me up like that with such ease. I'm terrified. I know I can't fight him, though. I would never free myself from whoever this is. He puts me down on the ground. I try to stand up, but a shout stops me: "GET BACK DOWN! NOW!" The powerful sound's muffled, but somehow oddly familiar.

"Ok," I whimper. My voice comes out much weaker than I want it to. I practically whisper. I'm back down on the ground now, crying. I hear a whisper that sounds like a "sorry" in that same gruff voice. The man then kicks me, and I fall into a hole. I'm a teary mess. My eyes are so blurry, I can't see anything besides my hands on the ground beneath me. Before I can even comprehend what's happening, a lid is placed quickly on the box into which I fell. Rocks and dirt begin to fall on it, and I realize I'm being buried alive, and there's nothing I can do about it!

I've been very claustrophobic my entire life, and now I'm being shut up in a box and buried alive. That's ironic. I desperately beat at the lid of the box, I scream at the top of my lungs, I scratch and kick and claw, but nothing makes any difference. Finally, the sound of the falling dirt stops, and I am beginning to come to terms with just how bad this is. There is no way I can ever escape. If I hadn't been so nosy, if I hadn't butted into my father's business, if I had been a better daughter, none of this would've happened. If I hadn't found those bills, I would probably be asleep in the comfort and safety of my own bed right now. I am so stupid.

I have to snap out of it. I can't just sit here and do nothing, feeling sorry for myself. I scoot down to the bottom of the coffin, or at least as far as I can go, and position my feet on the lid. I kick as hard as I can with both feet, and I feel a shift. I'm so close to getting it open, so close. I kick again, and this time, the lid pops off. I dig through the dirt until I make it to the surface of the earth. I pull myself out of the tiny hole and fling myself on the ground, gasping for air. Before I have time even to think about how exhausted I am, I run back to my house. Not just running – I'm sprinting. It's as if my body is on autopilot, and I can't control my legs. I finally reach my house, but as I walk in, I hear a noise. I look around while still panting from running so fast. I catch a glimpse of a shadow slithering across the yard and passing through the backdoor. I look over and can't believe my eyes. I see my uncle, carrying a black mask and a shovel covered in dirt.

4. What Lies Beyond The Field
By Izabella Felts and Gabriel Gerometta

Hi, I'm Allan, and this is the story of how my friends and I got into a mess we will never forget. It all started the summer before eleventh grade when I, my girlfriend Alyssa, and my best friend Frederick were hanging out in the field by my house.

"It's getting dark. I think we should call it a night," Alyssa said with disappointment.

"Yeah, I agree," Frederick and I said in unison.

"Jinx!" I yelled. Frederick snarled at me.

"Come on now. Stop giving each other death stares," Alyssa lectured.

"Okaaay," I replied.

All of a sudden, we saw something dashing through the woods beside us. It wasn't that noticeable until we were about to go inside. Then, before we knew it, we were darting through the wheat field, stumbling over the sticks and holes that were made by the animals of the night. Once Alyssa and I let Frederick catch up at the edge of the woods, we all went in, not knowing what we were getting ourselves into.

We went to the edge of the woods, with food and water packed for our adventure, around ten o'clock. The autumn leaves were falling and the grasshoppers chirping, performing their songs. We didn't notice anything unusual going on. We were starting to go back after this disappointment when we heard the leaves rustling behind us.

"D-did you all hear th-th-that?" whispered Frederick.

"Don't be scared. It was probably just a rabbit or something," Alyssa reassured him.

Then, out of nowhere, a hand pulled us into the darkness. A hand that changed the entire course of events.

"Ahhh!" we screamed.

I hit my head on a rock while being pulled in and passed out.

When I woke up, I was lying on the ground, looking at my surroundings.

"Ouch!" My head felt like it had been pounded with a jackhammer.

A little bit later, Alyssa and Frederick both woke up as well. We looked around, and none of us knew what was happening. I could tell from the looks on their faces. All I knew was that we weren't at my house anymore.

"Where in the world are we!?" asked Alyssa.

"I dunno, but this place is giving me the creeps," I responded.

"All I know is that this place is really freaking me out!" Frederick cried.

Then, as I turned my head, I spotted something in the distance. It looked like an animal, but it also looked like a human standing on its skinny legs. It had brown flesh with dark red eyes. Those eyes brought fear and terror to me, but I didn't know why.

Somehow, I knew it wasn't human, like one of us. Then, out of the blue, it charged straight at us!

"Guys, we have to run. NOW!" I exclaimed.

We bolted through every path we could. We ran faster and faster and faster until our arms and legs were sore. Then we found another path to run on, and eventually lost the beast.

"Whew! I think we lost it," I panted. "However, it seems we're lost."

"Yeah, but we ran too much!" Alyssa complained

"Wh-what was that thing?" Frederick asked, frightened.

"Good question. What was that thing chasing us?" Alyssa responded.

"I don't think anyone is going to know the answer to that question, but something tells me that this 'thing' is dangerous," I explained.

We wandered around for about an hour until we figured out something wasn't right. It seemed that we were walking in a circle.

"Ughhh... we've been walking for so looong," whined Alyssa.

"That's strange. It does feel like we've been walking for a while," I agreed. So, we traced our steps to what we thought was the beginning and figured out something that changed our entire mindset.

"I know this might sound unsettling, but I think we're going in circles," I started. "Every time we go a different way, we end up in the same place."

"You're right," Frederick agreed.

"What are we going to do?" I asked.

"I have no idea, but we are going to get through this together," Alyssa said with confidence.

Frederick suggested that we rest for a while, then try to make a plan. That was when our adventure truly began.

About thirty minutes passed, and nothing came to our minds. Then, I thought of something.

"What if we try to kill the beast?" I suggested. "It's dangerous, but this will probably be our only chance."

"Wait! What if that thing eats us alive!" Frederick asked.

"Let's keep exploring for now. We might find something to kill that creature with. Something other than your rusty knife, Allan!" Alyssa pointed out.

"Hey! That was my grandfather's knife! He gave it to me before he died!" I replied.

"Wait, did y'all hear that?" Frederick asked.

"No, what did you hear?" Alyssa replied.

"Someone or something is crying, and I don't want to know where it's coming from," Frederick explained.

"Wait, there's someone else here? If there is, we need to find that person," Alyssa argued.

"But what if it's that monster trying to lure us into one of its traps?" I whispered.

"We have to find out. It's better to take the risk so that there will be more people on our team," Alyssa suggested.

Frederick finally agreed to investigate the crying. Maybe another person would be able to help us get out of this situation.

Then, we were off, trying to figure out which direction we needed to go. The crying hadn't stopped yet, which was good because it made navigation much easier. After an hour or two, or maybe even three, we made it.

There was a girl holding a lifeless body in her pale arms. She had beautiful white hair and a delicate face. After a few minutes of awkward silence, she finally got up and introduced herself.

"H-Hello," she stuttered.

"Your hair... it's beautiful," Alyssa said in awe.

We were all puzzled by how white her hair was. Her hair resembled the feathers of a swan. It was sad to see her like this, with a dead corpse in her arms.

I was curious who it was, so I asked, "Who is this poor soul?"

"He was my brother. He...was killed by the b-beast," she said while looking at us.

A tear then rolled down her face.

"He was the only person I had left," the girl said, now sobbing.

"It's going to be alright," I reassured her. "What's your name?"

"Elanor. Elanor White," she answered.

Then, we heard a roaring in the distance. Whoosh! The beast rushed towards us. Boom! Its arm pounded into the floor and created a garden of deadly, black flowers. After most of the flowers bloomed, they emitted pollen that looked deadly to breathe.

"Hold your breath!" Elanor shouted. "Those flowers may be pretty, but their pollen is toxic to inhale!"

"Are you sure?" Frederick asked.

"Yes! This happened before when I was trying to fight the beast! I passed out, but my brother gave me time to escape!" Elanor replied.

They continued to sprout around the wood-like maze as we ran for our lives. Then, out of the corner of my eye, I saw a gleaming chest with something peculiar inside: a sword, shining in all its glory, grace, and beauty.

"We need to get that sword!" I explained. "That's the only thing that will get us out of here!"

"Frederick, go left! Alyssa and Elanor, distract it! I'll get the sword!" I yelled.

Everyone agreed to the plan, and we split up. We ran like the wind, the others trying to divert the beast's attention from me. Elanor ran in circles while Alyssa yelled at the beast to draw it away. I ran to get the sword and was flung into the air along with it. I caught the gleaming beam of light, slid onto the beast's arm, jumped up to its head, and then stabbed the sword into its heart. The beast wailed in despair as it lost its battle. Finally, the beast started to wither away, bleeding from the gash in its chest. It collapsed and spent its final moments howling in pain.

After the fight, we started to feel a strange rush of adrenaline through all of us. It was like an instinct that something was about to happen.

"What's happening!" we all yelled in unison.

Poof! We had disappeared from the loop and landed back at the edge of the woods, where we stood confused. This was where we had gotten ourselves into trouble a while ago.

"Thank goodness we're back!" Alyssa cried.

"Yes, I agree," responded Elanor.

"Wait, something doesn't feel right," Frederick added. "Allan, what time is it?"

"Hold on just a second. My phone's right here...," I began.

"It's 10:30," I said.

My friends were puzzled.

"That can't be right!" exclaimed Frederick.

"Where we were in that place, time in our world must have stopped," Elanor explained.

We hadn't been gone long enough for my worried parents to come looking for us.

After saying our goodnights, Elanor went home; she hadn't seen her parents for about five years. I thought she might start going to our school!

I needed to get some rest because Mom said there's a football game tomorrow. Thank you for letting me share this story with you all.

"That sounds like an adventure, Allan!" Mrs. East, Allan's eleventh grade teacher, said with a smile. "Next student is...Elanor! Will you please tell us what you did over the summer,"

"Oh, yes! It goes a little something like this..."

5. A Thin Line Between Love and Death
By Jasmine Gauvin and Kyannah McDonald

Let me tell you a story about love, death, and tragedy. It all happened when I met the new girl at my school. Ever since then, my life hasn't been the same.

"Dominic Jones, please come to the office. I repeat, Mr. Dominic Jones, please come to the office." I heard the announcement as I was going to first period.

As I made my way up to the office, I saw a beautiful girl standing there. I wondered what she was doing. I opened the door and saw the girl had a little sticker on her shirt that read "Hi, I'm new here." God, I hated wearing that thing when I was new. Now I feel bad for the poor girl.

"Hi, Mr. Jones. This is Ms. Amber Webb. She's new, and we want you to show her around to all her classes," the principal told me.

"Ok. Well, I'm Dominic. I guess I'll be your tour guide," I introduced myself.

She just gave me a short nod then handed me her schedule. As I looked over it, I realized we had all the same classes except for rotation; she had band instead. *I wonder what she plays?* I thought to myself.

"Well, we pretty much have the same schedule, so you can just follow me after I show you to all your classes," I said as we started walking down the hall.

"'K," she replied shortly.

Ok, she's not much of a people person, or she's just rude, I thought to myself. *I guess time will tell.*

As we walked through the halls trying to find the first classroom, I noticed she was wearing a shirt with my favorite band on it and many bracelets. *Cool, maybe we might have some things in common after all.*

"Nice shirt. Do you listen to them?" I questioned, trying to make conversation.

"Yeah, they're my favorite band. Do you know them?" she asked with an excited face.

"Yeah, they're my favorite, too. Actually, I got to see them a few years ago in concert. It was amazing!" I replied with enthusiasm.

"Man, that's awesome. I wish I could do something like that. I just don't have the money to go to a concert," she said with a sudden air of sadness.

Just when everything went quiet, we arrived at the first classroom I was supposed to show her. When I peeked in, I realized this was Ms. Hope's planning period, so I decided to introduce Amber to Ms. Hope. I knocked and heard a faint "come in" before I slowly opened the door.

"What are you doing here, Dominic? Aren't you supposed to be in first period right now?" Ms. Hope asked.

"Oh, I'm showing the new student around." I turned around and didn't see anyone behind me. "Amber, where are you?"

I stepped out of the room and saw her looking at a paper on the bulletin board. As the light shined through the window, I saw that there were tears in her eyes. I walked over, wondering what she had seen that made her tear up. It was just a paper. What could be so bad? When I arrived at the board, I saw what she was looking at. It was a suicide awareness poster.

"Hey, Amber, are you ok? What's wrong?" I asked quietly.

"Yeah, I'm fine. It's nothing." She sniffled as she started to walk to Ms. Hope's classroom.

"You know, you can talk to me. I'm always here if you need me," I said.

She nodded and walked by, dismissing me.

The rest of the day was similar. I would talk, and she would dismiss. I didn't know what I had done wrong, but at the end of the day, she finally talked to me again instead of ignoring me. However, she said something I didn't expect.

"Hey, I'm sorry about how I've been acting. I...It was just the poster that made me upset. I'm sorry," she said with her head hung low.

"It's okay. I understand. I tend to give the silent treatment when I'm upset too, so no biggie," I told her.

As the weeks went on, we became closer and started to talk more. The more we talked and got to know each other, I started to like her as more than a friend. Although I was far too afraid to tell her, all I could think was *What if she doesn't like me back? What if it ruins our friendship?* I didn't like the thought of just being friends, but I couldn't bear the thought of not being friends at all. I ended up going against my better judgment and decided I would tell her.

As I went into school on Monday, I was dead set on telling her, but as I went to find her, I noticed she wasn't at school. I wondered where she was. I hoped she was okay. To ease my worry, I pulled out my phone and texted her. After three hours with no reply, I finally decided to give up.

The next day, I saw her walking in the hallway.

"Hey, Amber, why weren't you at school yesterday?" I asked as I walked up to her, noticing she looked sad. She kept pulling down her sleeves.

"Oh hey, Dom. I...I was s-sick. Yeah," she said, as if she were trying to convince herself that was true.

"Okay, why didn't you reply back to me?" I asked, knowing she was lying. The only thing I couldn't understand was why she was lying to me.

"Oh, I didn't see that you had texted," she said as she pulled her phone out and acted like she was looking to see where I had texted. What she didn't realize was that I could see where she had seen the thread yesterday, so I knew she was lying. I didn't want to push her, though, so I let it go. Little did I know this would be the worst mistake of my life.

The morning went on as usual. Amber sat by me in first and second periods. We then split for third. Although we sat together all morning, we barely spoke, and it seemed like Amber was trying to hide something from me. She was very distant and seemed stressed. I didn't know what was wrong, but I wanted to get to the bottom of it.

As third period came to an end, my rotation teacher let me out early, so I went by the band room to wait for Amber. I saw her practicing with the other flutes in one of the closets. She was showing the rest of her section how to play a beautiful piece. She seemed very peaceful as she played. It was as if she were in a different world. As she stopped, the bell rang. All I could do was stand there, mesmerized by her playing. When she noticed me, she started blushing and packed her stuff away quickly.

While we started to walk to our next class, I couldn't stop myself from saying something about her playing. "That was beautiful, Amber. I've never heard anything like that before," I said in amazement.

"Thanks, Dom, that really means a lot, even if it's not true," she replied with gratitude, but also with a hint of insecurity.

I grabbed her by the hand and stopped her. "Don't say that, Amber. You were amazing. That was the most beautiful thing I've ever heard," I urged, taking her face in my hands.

She just looked at me as we stood there, my hands still holding her face. My eyes searched her face. Just then, I noticed her blushing and looking at my lips. It was as if we were gravitating towards each other, and the air was getting thicker. Before I knew it, Amber' lips touched my lips. Surprise set in, and I didn't kiss her back. Amber pulled back and ran away.

Still in shock, I just stood there and watched her run down the hall. As I processed what had happened, I started to run after her. I looked throughout the hallway but couldn't find her.

Where could she have gone? I thought to myself as I kept searching. Finally, I came across a janitor's closet and heard crying coming from inside. That must be her.

I opened the door to the closet and saw her sitting in the corner having a panic attack. I couldn't help but laugh because the mop was behind her and it looked like she was wearing a wig. She looked up, the hurt evident in her eyes. I could tell it was because I was laughing. *She must think I'm laughing at her.* I knelt down to her level and grabbed her hands to calm her down.

"Amber, why are you crying? It's ok. Everything is ok. You didn't do anything wrong," I tried to comfort her.

"I shouldn't have done that, I'm so sorry. I'm so, so stupid. Why would I do that?" she started rambling.

I wrapped my arms around her, trying to stop her from crying. Finally, after about ten minutes, I got her to calm down. As her breathing steadied, I began to pull away. Looking her in the eyes, I saw her panic.

"Amber, I have something to tell you…" Before I could finish, she cut me off.

"Please don't do this, I didn't mean to. Please don't leave me. I can't live with the thought of being left again, please," she said with earnestness and sorrow, her words running together.

"Amber, I'm never going to leave you. Please believe me when I say this. I love you so much, way more than I thought I could. I was going to ask you out, not leave you, Amber," I replied with a little nervousness, scared of what she was going to say.

"W-what? Why would you say that?" she questioned in disbelief.

"Because I like you, and you're really pretty and cool, and I love being around you," I started to ramble.

She just sat there looking at me in shock, mouth agape. As we sat there in silence, I started to worry. *Why would I do that when she was so distraught?* I thought to myself. I struggled to find something to say to her.

"Please say something, Amber," I mumbled.

"I just don't understand. Why me? I'm nothing," she said in confusion and sadness.

"Because I love you, Amber. You're the most beautiful thing I've ever seen, and you're so smart and funny," I replied earnestly.

"Ok," she said with confidence.

"What do you mean 'ok'? Is that a yes or no?"

"Yes. It means yes," she said as she jumped at me, grabbing my neck in a bone-crushing hug.

After that, the day went on as normal. Everything was amazing. We both laughed and had fun the rest of the day.

However, after Amber got off the phone in sixth period, she seemed a little off. She said that she didn't have a way home today so she would have to walk. When I tried to offer her a ride, she declined and said it was fine, that she would just walk.

Out of concern for her, I followed in my car. I saw her turn into the bad neighborhood and began to worry. *Is this where she lives? Why wouldn't she tell me? Does she not trust me?* All these thoughts ran through my head, making it hard to drive as I rushed home.

I couldn't sleep that night because of all these thoughts. I was struck with a sense of guilt and hurt. I was hurt that she didn't trust me enough to tell me where she lived. Then, I felt guilty because I had followed her home without her knowing. Why didn't she tell me? Did she think I would judge her?

The next morning, I was exhausted. Not getting any sleep last night caused me to move slowly this morning. When I was finally on my way to school, I decided that I was going to talk to her about where she lived, and find out why she didn't tell me. Just as I was rounding the corner, I saw Amber. This is my chance to talk to her before school.

"Hey, Beautiful," I shouted, trying to get her attention.

She didn't look back but, instead, started walking faster. *Did I do something wrong?* I thought to myself. The closer I got to her, the faster she walked. I stopped my truck and got out to catch her. As I caught up to her, I grabbed her by the shoulders and spun her around. As I looked into her beautiful green eyes, I realized they were closed.

"PLEASE DON'T HURT ME!" she cried out as I turned her around.

Just then, I realized there was a huge bruise on her face. Oh my gosh, what happened to her? Did someone do this to her? I had to know. She slowly opened her eyes, a look of relief and fear in them.

"Amber, what happened? Who did this to you?" I questioned with worry.

"N-nothing, I just walked into a door, that's all," she said unconvincingly.

I knew she was lying through her teeth, and I wasn't going to let her get away with it this time. No matter how hard I had to push her, I was going to get the truth. "Bee, tell me what happened. Please. Don't push me away again. I need to know the truth," I urged.

She just stared at me with a look of fear in her eyes. The longer I looked at her, the more noticeable were the little cuts and bruises all over her face. How could I have not seen them before. The more I thought about it, I realized I'd never seen her without long sleeves and jeans. There were so many things to be worried about.

"Please don't tell anyone, Dom. They will kill me," she sobbed as she clung to my shirt.

"Who will? Tell me who did this to you, Amber."

"It doesn't matter, Dom. You can't do anything about it. It is what it is," she replied in defeat.

I couldn't let this go, though. We both got in my truck to drive the rest of the way to school. I couldn't keep my thoughts from running wild. What happened? Who did this to her, and why? Was it her parents, a bully, a friend? Why would anyone want to hurt her? She is so beautiful and innocent. Why would someone want to break that? With all these thoughts flowing through my head, I started to get a headache.

As I parked the car, Amber asked me something I didn't expect. "Are you mad at me?" Her voice quivered as she spoke.

I parked the car, grabbed her face, and answered, "Why on earth would I ever be mad at you, Amber? You didn't do anything wrong, Bee. If anything, I'm sorry this happened to you."

After that, we went into school. I just couldn't focus the rest of the day, knowing someone had done this to Amber. She seemed so distant all day until sixth. She acted like she didn't want to leave me, almost like she was scared. So, I told her she could come and spend the night with me instead of going home. She agreed.

I drove us back to my house. Since it was the weekend, I told her she could stay till Sunday, but she refused and said she would go home tomorrow. We had the best time watching movies, eating popcorn, and dancing together. She looked truly happy for the first time since I'd met her, her long, brown hair in a ponytail and her green eyes shining as she laughed. All I could do was wish this night would never end.

The next day, I offered to take her home, but she said she had to go somewhere first, which I knew was a lie. Even though I knew she didn't have anywhere to go, I still let her walk away, knowing her house was only a few minutes from mine. Little did I know, this would be the last time I saw her.

When I went to school Monday, I had a really bad feeling. As soon as I walked into school, I looked for Amber, but she was nowhere to be found. Getting scared, I texted her, hoping for the best, but after thirty minutes without a response, I left school to find her. I sped to her house to see if she was ok. When I got there, the door was unlocked, so I went in. Looking around, I found a locked door that I could only assume was Amber's room.

I called out for her but got no answer, so without a second thought I broke it down. What I saw was something I would have never imagined. Amber's body was lying on the ground, lifeless, her blood all around, and a razor blade lying near her. All I could do was run to her and fall to my knees. I couldn't even move. I just sat there on the floor, holding her body. I was in such shock I couldn't even call the ambulance.

All of a sudden, I heard screaming and crying. What I didn't realize, though, was that it was coming from me. It was like I wasn't in my body anymore. Then, someone rushed into the room. Everything was happening in slow motion. At least, that's what it seemed like. In a distant voice, I heard someone on the phone with 911. All I could do was look down at Amber, lying in my arms.

Before I knew what was happening, I was being pulled away from her, and she was put in the ambulance. It felt like my heart was being ripped out of my chest. I couldn't deal with everything that was happening. I started throwing things, anything I could reach, and yelling. "WHY? WHY DID SHE DO THIS?" I screamed as I was throwing the contents of her room. Next thing I knew, someone was giving me a shot of something, and then I passed out.

As I woke up, I saw blinding white lights. *Where am I?* I thought to myself. As I was looking around, I realized that I was in a hospital room. *Why am I here?* All my questions were answered when a doctor came in.

"Do you know why you're here, Dominic?" the doctor asked as she walked in.

"No, not really," I replied.

As the doctor explained what had happened, I broke out in tears. I didn't understand why she would do this to herself. Why would she do this to me? The more I thought about it, the more I began to panic. All of a sudden, I couldn't breathe. I jumped out of the bed to try to walk around. When I stood up, I started freaking out, the realization just now setting in. I would never see her again.

I started throwing things and yelling again. "WHY WOULD SHE LEAVE ME? I LOVED HER! SHE WASN'T SUPPOSED TO LEAVE!"

The next thing I knew, I was waking up again, but this time in a room with nothing in it but myself and a mirror. "Where am I now?" I thought out loud.

"You're in the psych ward," answered a woman from behind me. When I turned around, there was a woman standing in the doorway.

She brought in a wheelchair and wheeled me out to where everyone else was. As she wheeled me to the common area, I heard a song playing. It sounded familiar. The more I paid attention, I realized it was the first song Amber and I had ever danced to, and it brought me peace. It gave me a sense that everything was going to be ok.

Then, the nurses took me to a room by myself. They gave me a letter that Amber had written to me before she had died. They left the room, giving me time to read it. As I opened the letter, a picture fell out. The first picture we had taken when I asked her out. I took the letter out and started to read.

By the first line, I was already crying. It was the most heartfelt thing I had ever read. The last line was what really stuck with me. "Everyone says there is a thin line between love and hate, but I disagree. I feel there is a fine line between love and death, because you give up everything for love, and lose everything in death. I gave you my love and lost you in death. I love you, Dom—Yours truly, Bee."

After that, I was released, I decided to live my life for Amber, doing her favorite things and living for her, going to the places she never got to visit. Now, every time I hear our special song, I think of her.

This story may have been full of love, death, and tragedy, but it also taught me to take chances and love fully...because you never know what could happen next.

6. Smokey Mountain Mystery

By Hunter Farley, Camden Russell, and Payton Wix

It was the middle of October when a group of friends had the idea to go to the Smoky Mountains for a month. Jayson was a good friend and really bright. Damien was quiet and sometimes looked depressed. Brody and Gunner were twins who both had strengths and weaknesses. Peter was active, but not bright. They rented a white van and were on their way. The group was halfway there when they stopped at a gas station. Jayson got out of the van to pump gas. The man at the other pump looked very odd. He was wearing a dark trench coat, black pants, and leather shoes. Jayson got a weird feeling when he looked at him. It was like the man did not even want him to know him.

They left the gas station thinking that the man was just a suspicious-looking character. They were back on the road, but ten minutes later, they saw the same man in the distance. They stared at him, but when they looked away, he was gone.

"This is weird," Gunner thought. Damien just minded his business.

They kept driving thinking it was just a coincidence. Then, all of a sudden, they lost control while driving over a river. They were scared for their lives. Jayson, being bright, took the wheel, but there was no point. They were heading over the bridge.

"What are we going to do?" Brody said nervously.

"Jump!" Damien replied. Unwillingly, they jumped out of the van and landed in the water. SPLASH!

They jumped out in the knick of time. They watched the van go into the river. They called an Uber to make it the rest of the way. Peter was traumatized and did not want to go to the cabin. However, the rest of the group insisted.

Jayson said, "We can still have a great time."

The friends made it to the cabin without any more problems, surprisingly.

"At least we did not see that weird guy again," Peter said.

Jayson thought, "That man was a little weird. He might return."

Peter sat in his room, scared. "Who was that man? What happened to our van?" he questioned himself.

Damien sat on his bed, not phased by anything that had happened. Brody and Gunner were fighting, thinking the other had caused this.

They went to bed that night, but Jayson did not. He wanted to investigate the crash. He knew it was not a coincidence. So, he returned to the bridge. While investigating the crash scene, he realized there were marks on the road.

"Something may have fallen out of the car, or possibly, a tire may have fallen off," Jayson thought as he went to bed that night.

Peter woke up early the next morning. He went outside to sit in peace. When he sat down, he heard a noise coming from the woods. It got closer and closer until it eventually stopped. Very curious about the noise, he couldn't resist the urge to check it out. Peter went closer, following the mysterious sound.

The others woke up two hours later.

"Where's Peter?" Brody asked.

"I do not know," Jayson said, confused.

They split up and started investigating outside. Brody walked to the edge of the woods and found Peter's boot.

"Hey, guys, I found Peter's boot!" he said.

The group wondered what had happened to Peter. They were worried sick.

"Guys, I don't feel safe anymore," Damien said.

"We could file a missing person's report," Jayson suggested.

"I think we should try to find him," Brody said.

"It's whatever we want to do as a group. I think it would be safer to file a report." Gunner said.

"But what would Peter want us to do?" Damien said.

"What if he is in danger and needs our help?" Brody added.

"I think we should go find him," Damien said.

The group agreed with Damien. They decided to go find Peter. However, after hours of tireless searching in the woods, they found nothing. They thought he was dead.

"Why did he have to die on this trip?" Brody asked with tears rolling down his face.

"I don't know," Jayson replied. They went to bed that night, sad about Peter's death. The next morning, Peter was back. They were overjoyed, but also confused.

"Where did you go, Peter?" Jayson asked.

"I was minding my own business until I heard a strange noise," Peter said in confusion.

"It doesn't matter, as long as you're safe," Damien said.

They went back inside the cabin, glad that their friend was safe. That night, they slept with no worries about their safety. Peter had trouble going to sleep that night.

Damien asked him, "What really happened to you yesterday?"

Peter was too scared to answer the question. He ignored Damien.

They woke up the next morning and rented a car. Brody and Gunner went to get groceries. They were on their way to the store when the mysterious man appeared in the middle of the road. They came to a halting stop.

"Who is that?" Brody said.

The mysterious man walked up to the car. He touched the car, and it vanished.

Back at the cabin, Jayson and Damien wondered where Brody and Gunner were.

"They should be back by now," Damien told Jayson.

"Yeah, I hope everything is okay," Jayson said worriedly.

They were beginning to fear that something bad had happened.

"Should we try to call them?" Jayson asked.

"There is no service out here," said Damien.

"Guys!" said someone in the distance.

When Damien and Jayson went outside to check it out, they saw Brody and Gunner.

"Guys, we saw a really strange guy on our way to the grocery store," Gunner said.

"What did he look like?" Damien asked.

"We couldn't see his face, but he was wearing a dark trench coat, black pants, and leather shoes," answered Brody.

"Hey, we saw that guy at the gas station on the way here," Jayson said confused.

"What if he's after us?" Peter nervously asked the group.

In the next moment, the power went out. The group could not see a thing, but they heard a blood-curdling scream. They were scared for their lives. When the power cut back on, Peter was missing, but there was a letter on the floor.

I took one of your friends. Let's play a game. If y'all do not come and save him by midnight, you will never see your friend again.

– Unknown

The group was scared.

"We cannot let Peter die," Damien said.

They nodded in agreement.

"We can save him and make it out alive, I know we can," Jayson said, confidently.

They left the cabin with the flashlights and wondered where Peter was. In the blink of an eye, they were knocked out.

They woke up in what looked like a dungeon.

"Welcome," a mysterious voice said. "You have exactly two hours until midnight to save your friend. If you can't find him in time, he will be hanged. Not only that, but you will die with him."

They were worried. They needed to save Peter, or they would all die.

"There are three rooms you need to pass through to save your friend," the mysterious voice declared. "You may enter whenever you choose, but you're losing time."

"We have no time to lose," Jayson told the group.

They entered the first room.

"The first room has four different ropes with four keys at the top. Only one key works, however," the voice again.

Brody was athletic, so he volunteered to climb the ropes. He climbed one rope and claimed its key. He took it to the door, but it didn't work. He climbed another rope and took possession of its key, but it didn't work, either. While climbing the third rope, he grabbed its key but then slipped. He hit his head and was knocked out. However, the key worked! His friends had to make a decision. Should they leave Brody behind and hope he followed, or should they drag him along with them? They entered the next room, dragging Brody behind them.

"You have completed the first room. The second room is tougher, though. There's a glass bridge with two pathways on each side. However, only one piece of glass can support your weight. If you pick the wrong one, you will fall to your death," the voice explained. "Good luck," it continued.

Brody said, "We should take turns trying the pathways," as he began to wake up from losing consciousness.

"I have a better idea," Jayson told the group. "We could use our shoes. We could test the strength of the different pathways by throwing our shoes on them."

The group liked Jayson's idea. When they were halfway across the room, Gunner slipped and fell to his death.

"NO!" Brody shouted. "WHAT HAPPENED?" he asked with tears pouring down his face.

"I don't know," Damien replied, also saddened.

"One of your group has died. Who will go next?" the voice asked gleefully.

They were able to cross the rest of the bridge with no further problems.

"You have lost one of your group, and you will lose another. You have thirty-five minutes left until you all die," the mysterious voice announced. "The last room contains an obstacle course. You might survive it, but probably not. So, you may avoid the course by sacrificing one of your own. The choice is yours. The course contains a swinging bridge, a rock wall, and a pit of piranhas. You may begin."

"We cannot sacrifice anyone," Jayson told the other two.

They agreed. They began the course by walking carefully along the bridge, but it still swung. At one point, it flipped, but the three friends hung on. They passed the bridge and went on to the 100-foot rock wall. Jayson started climbing but slipped. He did not fall too far, so he survived the accident.

About halfway to the top, they heard the mysterious voice say, "You have fifteen minutes. Better hurry!"

They looked at their watches, and it was right–they needed to hurry.

"Let's go!" Damien told them.

They made it to the top with ten minutes left.

They were then ready to face the piranha pit.

"I'll go in first," Brody told the other two.

Brody went in, and the others followed. Immediately, Brody was attacked by the piranhas. There was lots of blood in the pit. Jayson and Damien were also getting chomped, but they fought through the pain. Brody screamed in agony. Jayson and Damien made it to the other side with blood dripping down their arms and legs, but by then, Brody's screaming had stopped. Brody was dead.

Jayson and Damien had to keep going, and they entered the next room. They saw Peter, but the mysterious man had disappeared. They had thirty seconds left. They saw an opening in the wall.

"Do we go through?" Peter asked.

"There's no going back, or we will all die!" Damien told Peter.

They went through the opening. They had survived.

Damien, Peter, and Jayson walked out of the bunker.

"Thank you, thank you for saving me," Peter said.

"Yeah, it's just sad that we had to lose our friends," Jayson said.

"But they will never be forgotten," Damien said.

"Let's find a way out of here," Jayson said.

The three friends walked into the woods. A few minutes later, they got out.

"Finally, we made it out," said Jayson.

"HELP!" Peter cried to the passing cars.

One finally stopped.

"You kids lost?" the man in the car asked.

"Yes, can you help us?" Damien replied.

"Sure, get in," said the man. They got into the car and drove off, not believing what had just happened was real.

7. The Loop

By Adysen Glover

One Thursday afternoon, Allie was on her way home from school when Matthew, the boy she liked, drove his car next to the sidewalk. He proceeded to roll his window down and said in a happy voice, "Hey, Allie, you need a ride home?"

Allie exclaimed, "That would be nice, but I don't want to bother you."

Matthew then said, "Oh! You wouldn't bother me. I love talking to you."

Allie's whole face lit up and then turned red. She said, "If it's on your way home, I guess I could." So, Matthew got out of the car and opened the door for Allie. As she was getting in, she was nervously able to mumble, "Thank you."

Soon, the car ride was over, and Allie and Matthew had just arrived at Allie's house. However, something was different. The front door had been left slightly open, but Allie didn't think much of it because she thought maybe it just hadn't latched and the wind had blown it open. Then, she went into the house to her room. She sat her backpack down and went to grab a snack from the kitchen to hold her over till her mom brought home dinner. Next, she realized there was something on the table that wasn't there before. It was a letter that had been stamped with a red rose. It had Allie's name on it in bold letters, and Allie decided to open it to see if it was a late birthday card because her birthday had been only a couple of days ago. She opened the envelope and read: "Hey, Allie, I heard birthday was a few days ago through the grapevine or maybe your bedroom window. From your secret admirer." A little anxious, she thought maybe it was one of her friends playing a joke on her.

The next day when she went to school, she asked all of her friends. Finally, her best friend Amy said she had written the letter, and it was just a harmless joke. Relieved, Allie went home without worrying about finding another letter for her.

Once again, Matthew offered her a ride, and she accepted. This time, though, one of Matthew's friends decided to join, too. Allie was fine with that, hoping that Jacob, Matthew's friend, would break some of the tension between them. Luckily, Jacob started multiple conversations and helped them to get to know one another better.

Jacob asked, "Well, have y'all made it official yet?"

Matthew gave Jacob a weird stare because he didn't like feeling pressured, but that didn't stop Matthew from going on and on about his day. Allie's stop was first, and Matthew got out of the car to open the door for her, but as Allie was walking away, she heard from a distance, "Jacob, why would you put me on the spot like that? You know I'm going to ask her out tomorrow."

He then exclaimed, "I was just trying to get y'all to talk. Sorry."

Although Allie was a little worried about this conversation, she was also really excited about tomorrow because Matthew had just said he was going to ask her out. Allie was trying to find out what she would look best in for tomorrow. Then, her mom walked in, and they ate dinner.

Allie went back to looking for something to wear, and she heard her mom scream from downstairs "Allie!" She rushed downstairs and saw the television was on. Allie couldn't believe what she was seeing. The news lady was talking about a sixteen-year-old boy who had been murdered in Allie's town, but news lady never said who it was. Allie called Amy, because her dad was the sheriff and Amy was Allie's best friend, so she thought maybe she knew something. Allie's heart dropped at the news that Matthew, the boy who was going to ask her out tomorrow, had been murdered.

She went to the station as quickly as possible because Allie and Jacob had just been with him three hours ago. Once she got there, the police officers questioned her about everything that had happened that day. They even asked her to make a list of people who might not like Matthew. Sheriff Thompson said that Allie should come back the next day to see if they had any leads. "I will be back tomorrow," she told him. Then, she went to her car to cry.

She woke up the next morning and decided not to go to school because she thought it would be too much to deal with. She went down to get some breakfast and found the window open and a note once again lying on the table. She was too nervous to open it alone, so she took it to the police station. When she got there, she sat down with Sheriff Thompson, opened it, and read, "You were mine, you were my girl! Matthew couldn't just take you away from me. I've waited all this time for you and you can't just move on to someone new. Matthew stole your heart, so I had to steal his. Literally. Maybe now you'll fall in love with me the way you fell for Matthew because you won't have to worry about having to make a choice." Officer Thompson was in shock.

Allie was trying to think about who had written the letter, and then it dawned on her. He didn't do this just because he felt like killing someone. "He did it out of spite because he wanted me," she cried. Allie then returned home and tried to take a nap to get her mind off everything that had happened in the past couple days. However, when she woke up, her mom hadn't come home yet, which was unusual because it was 8 pm and her mom usually got home at 6. She didn't stress about it, though, because she thought with everything happening maybe her mom had fallen asleep in her car. That was until the next morning when her mom still wasn't home.

Once again, she went downstairs. And once again, there was a letter. She opened it and read, "Go check the mailbox, Sweetheart." Allie hurried to the mailbox and was shocked to see her mom's steering wheel on the ground next to the mailbox. She didn't understand at first, but eventually she heard from her best friend Amy that the rescue team had just pulled her mom's car out of the lake. Amy then said, "It's weird, though. The steering wheel wasn't there." Allie decided she should talk to Sheriff Thompson to get more details about the accident. Once Sheriff Thompson started explaining, it was obvious her mom's accident was no accident.

Allie then started to explain, "This morning I woke up and found another letter. This one told me that I needed to check the mail, and when I did, my mom's steering wheel was lying next to the mailbox." When the rescue team returned to the crime scene, they found Allie's mom strapped down to the seat and the brake pedal was missing. Allie figured this was the killer's doing.

When she arrived home, she didn't want to be alone, so she called Amy to ask if she could stay with her. "Yes, of course," Amy said, "there is no way you could ever stay alone at a time like this." Allie was relieved about not having to be alone, but she dreaded what tomorrow would bring because she had decided finally to go back to school. She knew everyone would be talking about the murders.

School went pretty well, at first. Of course, she was whispered about and pointed at, but that was not the worst thing. Just after third block, Allie went to her locker to get her history book. Her heart sank when she opened it, for there was another letter. She rushed to the bathroom, closed the stall door, and began to sob as she read, "Hey, Allie, it's me again. I know you missed me. I want you to listen very carefully. You're not gonna tell no one you got another letter. You're gonna continue your day as if nothing has happened. You're gonna meet me on the corner of Braxton Road, and you better not bring anyone else, if you value your life. You're gonna be a killer with me, and we're gonna be a power couple, and no one will ever come between us."

When she opened her stall door, she realized there were three other girls in the bathroom, and when they saw her, they ran. Allie didn't understand why they were running, but when she stepped out of the bathroom, she saw the big bold letters written on the wall of the hallway in red paint: "Allie is the killer. I saw her kill her own boyfriend down at the creek." It seemed accurate because that's where they found Matthew's body. Allie knew she wasn't the killer, but whoever wrote this must have been the killer because that's where they found the body.

Everyone must have really thought she was the killer, though, so she needed to run away. She ran to the woods behind her house because there was an old shack there where she could hide. It was about time to go meet the secret admirer, so she left in the dark, wearing all black.

However, when she got there, she was shocked to see Jacob. "What are you doing here?" she said, and that's when it hit her. It was Jacob! It made so much sense because he was the last one to see Matthew before he went missing.

That's when he started explaining himself: "All I ever wanted was you, but you never looked at me. It was always Matthew, and I thought maybe if he was gone, you would fall for me." Jacob started to get mad just thinking about it. However, Allie was confused about who had killed her mom because Jacob had been at practice from 6 to 8 that evening.

Something wasn't adding up, and she needed to figure out what it was. So, she said, "Why would you want us both to be killers?"

He answered, "So we would have something in common, something that would bond us together." Allie knew for a fact Jacob hadn't killed her mom. Someone had to be working with him. She decided she would play along, and hoped that by doing so she would find out the facts about her mom's murder. They began talking about people who they thought deserved to die, and that's when Jacob mentioned his old bully Tommy.

Later on, they went to find Tommy. That's when Jacob mentioned that his friend was going to join them.

"Who is it?" she asked.

"Calvin," he answered. She didn't really know Calvin that well, but her mom used to date his dad in high school. However, when her mom met her dad, she decided to break up with Calvin's dad. That made sense because it gave Calvin a motive.

Then, she said, "Can we go for Tommy tomorrow? It's been a long day."

The next day, when Allie woke up, she was a little confused. She had fallen asleep with Jacob, but now he was nowhere to be found. She decided to start getting ready for school, but when she went downstairs to get something to eat, her mom was there cooking breakfast. Unsure what to think, Allie grabbed some toast and then started her journey to school.

On the way back home that afternoon, Matthew drove his car next to the sidewalk. He proceeded to roll his window down and said in a happy voice, "Hey, Allie, you need a ride home?" This cycle repeated itself for the next five years. Allie was afraid ever to change her actions because she was scared of losing the people she loved the most.

Finally, after living in the loop for five years, Allie broke down and decided to change her future. Instead of taking the ride from Matthew on the first day, she asked Jacob to pick her up. Unfortunately, she messed things up even worse, for then her best friend Amy took the ride from Matthew, and Jacob rode with them the next day. She knew what was going to happen next, so she did what she had to do.

She followed Jacob until he arrived at Amy's house, and once Matthew and Jacob left there, she followed them to the creek. Then, right before Jacob was going to kill Matthew, she stepped in and killed Jacob.

Now, she had a bigger problem. She was the killer, and Matthew was trying to reach the police. She knew what she had to do. She killed Matthew so he wouldn't turn her in. Naturally, she panicked and regretted the decision, so she went to her house, lay down, and went to sleep hoping she would return to the loop. However, she didn't. When she woke up, there were police cars racing towards her house. She could hear their sirens. She'd finally escaped the loop, but she could never escape the consequences of her actions.

8. I Thank God
Kaylee Meador

Usually, after people experience something great in their life, they say that it was the "best thing that has ever happened to them." But they say it without really meaning it. However, I can say that about one thing in my life and really mean it. There is one thing that happened in my life that I will always remember as the best thing I have ever experienced.

It all started in 2021. I was in 6th grade, and I had been going through a lot mentally for a long time. I began to lose a lot of friends, and as time went by, I ended up with just a few people in my life. After a few more months, I started to question if any of them actually wanted me in their life at all. I always felt left out at every event I went to. I ended up teaching myself to stay silent and not speak to anyone, not even my own family, unless I had been asked a question. I thought no one really cared about me or what I had to say.

Soon, it was February of 2022, and 6th grade was almost over. One night, my brother and I went to visit my grandparents. As we were walking to the car to leave, I glanced at him and saw him jerk his neck. I thought nothing about it at first, but then he did it again. I decided to ignore it and not say anything until he said something I will never forget. He said, "Kaylee, I think I might have Tourette Syndrome," and then explained to me what Tourette's is (a neurological disorder involving involuntary tics, vocalizations, and sometimes the compulsive expression of obscenities).

It was pretty late, I was tired, and I didn't think before I responded. I replied, "No, you probably don't." This conversation escalated very quickly, turning into an argument. I accused him of faking tics, wanting attention, and more things that I shouldn't have said. This is definitely one of my biggest regrets. Even if I didn't believe him, I should have thought it through before saying all of those things. I had no idea that my life would be changed forever in just a few more weeks.

When we got home that night, I overheard him talking to my parents about it. I decided not to say anything and just go to bed. About a week later, he got home from work one day pretty late but still went to tell our parents good night. While in their room, he was jerking his neck, blinking very hard, and other things more than any of my family had ever seen before. It was so bad that our mom and dad even considered taking him to the emergency room in case he was having a seizure. This is when they decided to schedule a neurological appointment for him to see if he really did have Tourette Syndrome.

I did not hear about any of this until a few days later. I was sitting in the living room when my mom came and sat next to me. She said she needed to talk to me about something, and then she told me everything that had been happening. She told me something that may have been the most memorable news of my life, but not in a good way. She said that my brother had gone to the doctor and was diagnosed with a tic disorder. We didn't know if it was specifically Tourette Syndrome yet, but a few weeks later, we were assured that it was. I will never forget that moment. I was filled with regret. I felt incredibly bad for not believing him the night that I accused him of lying and only wanting attention.

That is when I reached the lowest point in my life. It tore my heart to shreds to watch my brother struggle so much with this incurable condition. He was put on many medications to try to calm his convulsions, but it got to the point that we couldn't even talk to him without being interrupted by multiple tics. They got so bad that some of them made him hurt himself or do rude things. This disorder was even keeping him from doing simple tasks.

One day that I remember very well, we were getting ready to eat dinner as a family. He was simply carrying his glass of water to the table, but his convulsions caused him to spill it. Later, one of his tics caused him to lift his phone up above his head like he was going to throw it across the room. I specifically remember him telling us he could not move, which broke my heart. Before he could throw it, we finally got his phone out of his hand.

At school, people were making fun of him and accusing him of faking. Tourette Syndrome was causing so many issues in his life while breaking my heart at the same time.

Soon, it was the end of June, and it was time for church camp. For the first few nights, my brother was doing pretty well. However, he was having a lot of trouble one day. My parents ended up bringing him my ukulele because he always loved playing it, and it really helped with calming down his tics. However, that was only temporary, so he still had some bad moments when he didn't have the ukulele.

The very last night of church camp was the night that changed my life. The service was going great already, but it wasn't any different from the other services we had at first. It was about to be over, but then, God started moving in amazing ways during worship after the message. Everyone was on the floor praying their hearts out, praising God, and it was all so beautiful. I was already empowered by the Holy Spirit like everyone else was that night, but then one of the songs really touched my heart. The worship team played the song "Rattle" by Elevation Worship. The lyrics say, "My God is able to save and deliver and heal, and restore anything that He wants to." This part of the song made me realize something that changed my life that night.

I realized how amazing and powerful God really is. To Him, anything is possible. He can cure the incurable. He is more than able. I was just in awe of how wonderful He was. Before, I didn't really understand why people loved Jesus so much or what was so great about God. The presence of God just overwhelmed me at that moment. *He could heal my brother.* I felt so different about life. I felt so different about everything. My perspective on the world changed, and I walked out of service that night feeling so purified and enlightened. I finally understood. I realized what our God is really capable of doing.

As I stepped outside after the service, I looked around me, and it was like the whole world became so much more beautiful. I looked into the sky, and instead of just seeing some stars against a black background, I saw an amazing canvas of God's wonderful work. I looked around me at all of the people at that camp, and instead of just seeing them as random people, I saw them as God's children. Later, all of the campers and leaders had a bonfire, and we were eating s'mores and singing worship songs. I was just amazed that I had never realized how powerful the Lord is and how amazing it is that He created everything that I see. I felt healed and loved like I had never felt before. It was a great awakening of my heart.

After church camp, I lived a completely different life. I tried my absolute best to read the Word of God every day and talk to Jesus every time I had the chance. Every time I prayed, I always asked God to help my brother and give my family peace. That was the most important thing to me other than pursuing God.

Eventually, after months had gone by, I hadn't seen much change at all with my brother and his Tourette's. I was starting to lose hope and wonder if God would ever actually make it better, but one night while I was praying, God revealed something to me.

I vividly remember Isaiah 40:31 going through my mind: "Wait on the Lord, and He will renew your strength." From that moment on, I never gave up on praying for my brother and praying for peace within my family.

Soon enough, there were some days that I even forgot he had Tourette Syndrome for a while. That was how much better it has gotten through my and others' prayers. God showed me who He is and just how mighty He is. And yes, there were times that my brother still had rough days with his Tourette's, but mostly, people he met would never have guessed that he had it.

By 2023, I had given my life to Christ forever. I put my faith in Jesus on December 14 of 2022. Since then, God has never let me down. Most people see following the Lord as limiting their life because of giving up sin, but if they only knew how freeing it truly is. I am free now, and I have a place in Heaven awaiting me. Now, I do everything I can to share my story and the gospel with others.

I was raised to believe in God my whole life, and my dad is even the pastor of our church. However, I never *really* believed so genuinely until I had an encounter with Jesus that one night at church camp. And as I mentioned, I didn't understand why people loved Jesus so much. I guess I just couldn't wrap my mind around what He did for me and everyone on this planet. Now I know that He loved us first. He loves us with a love far beyond what any mind could ever comprehend.

In summary, if you struggle with the same troubles I did or do not understand why Christianity is so great, just give God a chance with your life. Once you have an encounter with the Holy Spirit and feel God's presence, you'll never be the same. Let your perspective on life be changed. Seek the Lord, and He will do amazing work in your life. He healed my heart, and I will never forget it. Let Him heal yours, too. I am a completely different person than I was just a few years ago. I thank God.

9. Sleepover Gone Wrong!!!

Lydia Hunt, Katelynn Passic, and Kaylin Talley

Today is my birthday, and I'm having a sleepover at my house with all of my friends. I'm turning fifteen, and next year, I'll be able to drive! I'm really excited, if you can't tell already. Skylar, my best friend, showed up first, of course. Then came Campbell, then Bridgette. I had been waiting eagerly for everyone to arrive so we could hang out.

"I'm so excited!" Skylar screamed.

I smiled, and yelled, "Me, too!!"

We all went upstairs so they could set their stuff down. They looked around like they had never been here before, and I said, "Oh, we changed some things up here."

Skylar looked at me and said, "Yeah, I noticed."

I shook off that unnecessary comment and asked, "So...what do y'all want to do?"

They all looked at each other, and I knew exactly what they were going to say: "Volleyball!" So, we all headed back downstairs to put our shoes on.

Bridgette looked at us and slightly chuckled, "This is going to be bad. I haven't even picked up a volleyball in forever." We all laughed at that remark.

We headed out the door and found a flat space of land. "Ok, let's do this," I said.

We started hitting the volleyball around, and we were doing so well until...

"AHH! I'm so sorry guys," Bridgette said. "However, I did warn y'all that this wasn't a good idea to let me play."

We all looked at each other and smiled. "It's ok. I'm getting tired anyway," I said. We raced back inside, and of course, Skylar won.

We sat on my bed to watch TikTok, and I remembered something. Earlier, Skylar had sent me a TikTok about a scary trend, kinda like "Red Door, Yellow Door," and there were these people going out to the forest and awakening this spirit. Supposedly, if the seance is done wrong, the spirit possesses someone, and if the possessed one gets fully taken over by the spirit, the last person standing is stuck in the forest for eternity, with the spirit haunting that person forever. Doesn't that sound like so much fun?! I mean, I know it's all fake, but that's, like, the fun part about it. I also knew this was perfect because my backyard was a forest, so that TikTok was kinda made for us.

After we ate, it was nearing night. Skylar and I hadn't told anyone about the seance yet because we kinda wanted it to be a surprise. All of us were just scrolling on our phones like we always do, waiting for the night to come so we could start the party. When it was almost midnight, I texted Skylar to pull up the seance video and pretend like she had just seen it.

Skylar covered her mouth and said, "Guys, stop. We HAVE to do this tonight. Doesn't this look like so much fun?!"

The Perfect Couple and Other Stories

Skylar got up to show Cambell and Bridgette the phone. We gave each other a quick glance, knowing they would love this.

Campbell saw it and said, "Mmm...I don't know, that looks a bit sketchy, don't you think? I mean, what if it's actually true? No offense, Skylar, but I don't want to be stuck in that forest forever."

Bridgette looked at Campbell, then at me, and said, "I agree with Cambell. I'm also really scared of the dark, and Campbell's right. What if something bad really does happen?"

Skylar and I gave each other a "is-she-that-gullible?" look. Skylar looked at Bridgette and said, "That's the whole point, Bridgette!"

We all kinda agreed to do the seance, even though Campbell and Bridgette didn't really look like they wanted to, and we set our alarms for 3:15 am. We didn't really need to set our alarms, though, because we stayed up the whole night, watching the time on our phones, waiting for it to be at least 3:00 a.m.

Finally, it was time. We were all really excited. By 'we,' I mean me and Skylar. And we put our warm clothes on. It was kind of chilly outside, but not freezing. We snuck out as quietly as we could so my parents wouldn't hear and made our way down the stairs.

We were looking for a good place to start the seance. I turned to look at Campell and Bridgette to see how they were doing. Campell said, "Guys, are you sure you want to do this? This place is kinda freaking me out."

Skylar looked at her and replied, "Gosh, Campell, you're such a crybaby. You'll be fine."

Bridgette was kinda curled up next to Campell, and they looked really scared. "Maybe we shouldn't do this," I thought to myself.

We finally found the perfect little piece of ground to sit on. It was flat, and there wasn't any poison ivy on it. Skylar looked up the video again so we could remember how to do the seance. We lit up all the candles that we had brought down, we closed our eyes, and Skylar started the chant. We all held hands and followed her.

Skylar started: "nA Na nA nA Na Na."

We copied: "nA Na nA nA Na Na."

Then Skylar again: "nA Na nA nA Na Na!"

We again copied: "nA Na nA nA Na Na!"

I tried so hard not to laugh because of how funny this all was, but I kept my laugh in. When we finished, it was silent. We all let go of each other's hands and opened our eyes. When we did, Bridgette was gone. Campbell let out a shriek, and so did I. Skylar didn't, though. She looked, well...different.

I went over and held Campell to comfort her. I said to her, "It's ok. Maybe she got scared and ran inside or something, or maybe she ran back to her house. I mean, it's only a few houses away."

Campbell was in shambles, crying, "No, I felt her hand in mine the whole time! We are so deep in the forest, she couldn't have run that fast in the small amount of time since we released our hands! She's gone! Something must have gotten her! We should never have done this. I told you something bad was gonna happen!"

We all went back inside after Campbell stopped crying. Time had passed, and it was now 3:55 am. We looked around for Bridgette, but she wasn't there. Campbell almost had another breakdown until I saw Bridgette's stuff was gone. I told Campbell and then said, "Look, Bridgette's stuff is gone! She must have just gotten scared and run back inside to grab her stuff before she went home. See, she's fine!" That seemed to comfort Campbell a bit. We all decided to go to sleep. The seance trend must be fake, but it was still fun.

When I woke up, Campbell wasn't in her bed anymore. All her stuff was still in the house. *Maybe she just went to the bathroom*, I thought. I looked just to make sure, but she wasn't there. I was starting to get worried. On my way back to my room, I realized that the back door wasn't closed all the way.

As soon as I saw that, I bolted up the stairs and woke up Skylar. I was whisper-screaming and shaking her to wake up. She woke up looking groggy and said, "What do you want? Can't you see I'm trying to sleep?"

Gosh, since when was she so salty? I thought to myself. Then, using my inside voice, I said, "Campbell's gone!"

Skylar looked at me, but she really didn't look worried at all. She seemed unfazed by my words. "Ok, and...? What does this have to do with me?" she asked. I was shocked. Skylar and Campbell were not really the best of friends, but couldn't she show some concern? We just did a seance. What if that was real? What if something serious had actually happened to her?

"Skylar, why are you being so mean? You're, like, the nicest person I know. Why are you acting this way?" I asked.

"Because, Nevaeh, she's fine. You really think something like that could actually happen just because of some silly little Tik Tok trend? You are so naive," she replied.

"Skylar," I continued, "her stuff is still here, and she's not in the bathroom or anywhere else—I looked already. What if she went out to look for Bridgette?"

Now, Skylar looked worried. "Nevaeh, you don't think..." I stopped her before she could continue, I put on my jacket, grabbed hers, and bolted out the door, dragging her with me.

We reached the spot where we did the seance and started yelling both of their names. "Bridgette? Campbell? Where are you guys?" I shouted, and Skylar did the same.

We reached a narrow fork in the forest, and Skylar said, "I know this is what all the stupid characters in horror movies do, but we should split up and look for them—they're just movies, right?"

"I mean, I guess we could. Call me if you get lost and meet back here at 6:00 am, ok?" I replied.

"Got it," she said.

We split up and continued to yell, "Brigette? Campbell?" Where could they have gone?

It was reaching 6:00 am, so I started to head back to where I told Skylar to meet up if we couldn't find them. I called her when I was walking back. No answer. I called her again. Still no answer. Maybe she just had a bad connection or something. When I got to our meeting spot at 6:05 am, she was not there yet. I called her phone again. No answer. I started to get worried and shouted, "SKYLAR? *WHERE ARE YOU*!?" Was I out here by myself now?

I started to hear footsteps in the distance. "Skylar!" But I didn't see her light, beautiful blond hair, or her pretty, glowing face. Instead, the face was covered with black, dirty, knotted hair. And she didn't have her usual graceful, elegant walk. She was walking on all fours...creeping on all fours...running on all fours, right towards...me!

10. Schizophrenia: The Cycle

By Abbey Carter and Kiera Dyer

"Schizo! Breakfast!" Aunt Stacy called up the stairs.

"Coming!" I called back down as I slipped on my other heel and trotted down the stairs. I smelled the air when I walked into the dining room. My favorite, chocolate chip pancakes!

"Jesus, what took you so long?" my older brother, Jake, said with a smirk.

"Shut up," I snickered.

"You two behave back there," said my Aunt Stacy as she made me a plate.

"My bad, Aunt, we were just foolin'," said Jake, with the same stupid smirk on his face. He ran his fingers through his hair and started eating. I sat next to him and scarfed down my breakfast like a starving wolf. Aunt Stacy has always been a good cook.

"Hey, Aunt, why did Mom name me Schizo?" I asked after breakfast.

I could see the color drain from her cheeks, and I saw Jake look up from his phone with a confused and worried look. She sighed, and finally said, "You got your name from your mother's mental illness."

What? I knew my mother was diagnosed with Schizophrenia before I was born, but I guess I never connected the dots. "Why would she name me after her illness?" I asked. It just didn't make any sense to me.

Aunt Stacy sighed again and said, "Schizo, you and I both know she was crazy."

Jake looked back down at his phone, his hair covering his face. I hate to say it, but it was the sad truth. Dad worked so hard to keep a roof over our heads and food on the table, but Mom was unemployed and always abused me and Jake because her 'demons' told her to. She was fired from every place she worked for abusing the other workers. We were never able to get her help. Nothing worked. It was like the demons were actually there, but I knew they weren't real. "Yeah, I know," I replied.

I took a quick glance at the clock and rushed out the door. Today was prom. I wouldn't miss this for the world! The theme was White Raven, so there were lots of black and white decorations everywhere. They had white chocolate covered strawberries, dark chocolate covered strawberries, black velvet cupcakes, vanilla cupcakes with a cute chocolate raven topper, and black cake pops decorated to look like a raven. It was so beautiful! A couple minutes into the party, something happened. Why can't I breathe? What is happening?

Oh, it's just my asthma. I took out my inhaler, but as soon as I did, someone pushed me to the ground. Oh god, I knew he was going to be here. When I looked up, I saw the high school bully, Jason, laughing in my face. I couldn't hear anything but his sadistic laughter. So, so sadistic. I finally realized that when he pushed me, my inhaler flew out of my hands before I could do anything! He stepped over me, looked down at my inhaler, and stepped on it. I heard a loud cracking sound as it broke in half. I still couldn't breathe, and my face was frozen in shock. All I could hear was the cracking sound of the inhaler, then dead silence. Everything around me disappeared into an inky black darkness. I couldn't breathe, but it didn't feel important anymore, like I didn't need to breathe. I looked up and saw a pale face looking back down at me, its hair covering its eyes. All I could see was its extremely long black hair and its sharp-toothed smile stretching from ear to ear. It wasn't humanly possible to have a smile that big. Its mouth didn't move, but I swore I could hear a voice mumble something quietly, or maybe it was just my imagination.

My eyes shut tightly, and then opened a few seconds later. I was back at the prom, my inhaler in my hand, good as new. What! I could have sworn Jason had just broken it.

"Hey, Schizo!" I whipped my head around and saw Jason. No. I know what's about to happen. He slowly stepped forward. I'm not going to let him hurt me. I swung my fist and punched him in the throat. He fell to the ground, gasping for air. I watched him calmly. I looked ahead and saw Principal Jane running towards me. I was quickly suspended.

"That's all I can remember," I told my therapist, Dr. Xavier.

"Hmm, and what did this 'thing' look like?" he curiously asked.

"It had long black hair and pale skin, and it was very tall, roughly 12 feet tall. Its skin was strangely tight against its bones. I couldn't see its eyes, but it had an inhumanly large smile," I said.

"Interesting. You swore it said something?" he asked.

"It was probably my imagination," I said, uncertainly. It most likely was, but it felt so real, like it was actually there.

Just then, a shrieking sound came from behind me. I looked behind me quickly, frightened by the noise. The cuckoo clock squealed its cheery tune. "Oh, I'm afraid we are out of time. I'll see you Sunday, Schizo," Dr. Xavier said. I got up and walked out to Aunt Stacy's car.

A day went by, and nothing happened. I thought the 'thing' was just my imagination. Then, I heard a loud noise upstairs. What was that? It came from my brother's room. I bolted up the stairs to his room, scared for his life. Jake is my closest friend. I can't let something happen to him! I swung the door open as fast as I could, praying quietly that he was alright. The whole place was a mess. Wallpaper was torn off the walls, tables were knocked over; and his wardrobe was on the ground. I looked in the corner and saw Jake, sitting on the ground, rocking back and forth, his head in his hands. This wasn't like him. He was usually a pretty laid-back person, and he always kept his room clean. "J-Jake?" He mumbled some things. I couldn't tell what he was saying. I came closer, but he acted like I wasn't there. "Jake?" I said.

I heard the voice again. That thing was back. It walked past me and over to Jake, staring at him for a moment before plunging its bony arm right through him. He shook aggressively, like his soul was being ripped out of his body. I wanted to scream, but no sound came out. My eyes widened in fear before being forced shut again. When I opened them, the whole room was back to normal.

"Hey, Sis, what's up?" Jake's voice pierced through the silence like an arrow.

What? He's...back to normal? H-he was just–

"Schizo? You there?" he jokingly said, snickering a bit.

"Y-yeah, I'm fine," I said, trying to act as calm as possible. Something isn't right. *What is this voice doing? Is it...rewinding time and fixing everything? No, that's not possible...*

I decided to go to bed. I was tired and had had a long day.

I woke up in my parent's old house. I went downstairs to see my parents sitting on the sofa, watching TV.

"Morning!" they said almost in unison and with bright, warm smiles on their faces. I didn't smile back. Something inside me felt...angry. I didn't say anything and went to the kitchen, pulling a knife out of the knife block. Nice and sharp. I ran over to my parents and plunged the knife right through my mother's stomach. Once. Twice. Three times. I looked at my father. I stabbed him four times. Blood splattered on the walls. Their cold faces were frozen in shock. The perfect murder. I looked down at the knife. It was covered in blood, and so was I. I laughed to myself. I've always wanted to know what it was like to be stabbed to death. I held the knife close to my stomach.

Then, I shot up in my bed. I was sweating buckets. Tears flowed down my face as I thought of the terrible nightmare. I wiped my tears and got up. *It was just a dream, Schizo. Just a dream,* I said in my head. I went downstairs to get some breakfast. *Where's Aunt Stacy? She usually gets up pretty early.* I went to her room. "Aunt Stacy?" No answer. She was gone. I went to my brother's room. There was a note on his bed. I picked it up and read it aloud.

I'm so Sorry. I Can't deal witH this anymore. I'm tired of all this mIsery. I wish that Zomeday you will all find happiness and peace. Unfortunately, I can't. They taunt me. They torture me. I can't take it anymOre. I know what happened to Mom and Dad. Look by the lake.

The lake? Does he mean the lake next to our house? Why are some of the letters capitalized? Wait, do they spell something? I don't have enough time to figure this out. I have to see if my brother's okay; or even alive. I ran outside to the lake. Maybe Aunt Stacy will be there. If so, *why* is she there?

As soon as I arrived, my jaw dropped. Aunt Stacy wasn't there, but my brother was. He was floating on the lake with his mouth open. Water trickled down the side of his face. He was just floating on the water, like he was as light as a feather. He was dead. No, this isn't possible! What happened? Why did this have to happen? Tears streamed down my face like rivers. My closest friend, now gone.

The voice was back. I swear I heard it say my brother's name. I tried to scream, but I couldn't move. I felt its presence behind me. My eyes again closed tightly, and when I opened them, Jake's body was gone. Where did he go? Is he alive? I ran back inside. Aunt Stacy was looking around. What was she looking for?

"Schizo! There you are!" she exclaimed. "Where were you? Jake and I have been looking for you."

"Sis?" Jake exclaimed, in a somewhat excited and relieved tone, as he ran down the stairs. "You found her?!"

"Uh...um...I-I was outside," I stammered, still trying to process everything that's going on.

Aunt Stacy breathed a sigh of relief. "You had us worried there," she said finally.

Jake looked me up and down. "What were you doing out there? Did you get hurt or something? You have some blood on your shirt," he said, concerned.

I looked down. My shirt was stained with blood. What happened? "Uh, I just fell," I stammered.

"Come now. Let's get you cleaned up," Aunt Stacy suggested as she went upstairs. I started to follow her into the bathroom. "I'll get you some clean clothes and a bandage," she said, already halfway out the door. "I don't mean to scare you, but there's probably a pretty nasty wound under there for it to bleed *that* much."

"Thank you, Aunt," I said. I looked in the mirror, but instead of reflecting my face, the mirror was...pitch black? I climbed up on the counter and reached out my hand out to touch it, and my hand went right through the mirror. "Wh-What?" I said aloud in shock. I reached deeper into the inky, black abyss. My foot slipped, and I fell into the black void. What is happening? It was like black fog had obscured my entire vision. I looked around, and there it was. The thing that'd been talking to me all this time. It was so tall. Its inhumanly large smile looked almost fake, and its extremely long black hair covered its eyes, but I swore I could see tears. It extended its skinny arm and pointed to my right. I looked over, and I saw my parents' old house, the house they lived in before they died.

"Wh-what?" I whispered out loud.

"Go," it said, in an almost demanding tone. The voices of a raspy female and a warm-hearted male spoke in unison.

"Wh-why?" I yelled up at it so it would hear me clearly.

"The answers lie there," it called back down, still pointing to the house. Its mouth didn't move as it talked, and though I didn't hear its voice, I seemed to *sense* its voice was there. I walked towards the house. Random memories flooded my brain. Old memories.

I went inside, and I saw my parents. They were dead on the floor. I looked down, and found blood on my shirt. I had a sharp knife in my hand. "Mom? Dad?" I dropped the knife and walked closer. I picked up my mom's arm and checked her pulse. I felt nothing. "N-No...it's not true! I didn't do this!"

I turned around to see the thing staring down at me. "I'm sorry," it called down.

"Can you fix this? You fixed my brother! You fixed everything!" I screamed back up at it. I will never forget its response.

"You cannot fix your own regret. You did this to them. Now you will live through this misery over and over and over again. You *will* suffer for your actions. This is what you deserve."

The thing grabbed my wrist and said one word: "Reset."

My eyes were forced shut, until I heard my alarm clock screaming at me. I slammed my hand on the button to make it stop and sat upright in my bed. A new day. Was this a dream? It feels like I've experienced this before. Has this happened before? I brushed it off. It was probably just a dream. I got up, got dressed, and started slipping on my heels.

"Schizo! Breakfast!" Aunt Stacy called up the stairs.

"Coming!" I called back down as I slipped on my other heel and trotted down the stairs. I smelled the air when I walked into the dining room. My favorite, chocolate chip pancakes!

11. Gut Feeling

By Savannah Harrison and Annabella Hill

Last year, my girlfriend, Emma, went missing. They just found her a couple months ago. She was barely breathing, but she was able to explain what had happened.

Everything started when Emma and I went to my family's lake house together. We just wanted to get away from everyone for a few days. Emma and I had planned on staying there Monday through Sunday. However, on Wednesday things took a terrible turn.

When we arrived at the house on Monday, everything felt normal. Everything seemed to be in its original state, but as the day continued, we noticed some things were out of place. Some things from my childhood were even missing.

As we walked through the house, we realized there were dirty dishes in the sink. My sister Charlotte had been planning to bring some of her friends here for a girl's trip, so we thought it was nothing.

Emma did the dishes while I continued to walk through the house. We wanted to check the house because when we got there, the front door was unlocked, and our parents always made sure we locked the doors when we left. I wanted to check the house and make sure everything was okay, but I never noticed anything major.

After I finished walking through the house, we cleaned it up and started to unpack our things. We put away the food we had bought for the week. Then, we put our clothes away in the master bedroom.

After we got settled, I remembered that my family had left the jet skis on their trailers, so Emma and I decided to go for a ride. While we were out on the lake, I noticed something. There was what appeared to be the shadow of a person in one of the back windows. I quickly got back to the shore and ran into the house. As I approached the bedroom, I noticed a lamp was on that hadn't been before. The only issue was that there was no one in the room.

I never told Emma about the situation because I didn't want her to worry. She overthought everything, and I knew that if I told her, she would want to leave, and I didn't want to take that chance. I walked through the house every time I heard any noise that wasn't made by me or Emma, but I never found anything. The day seemed to go by pretty fast after that. I didn't notice anything again until that night, but I still had a gut feeling that something was wrong.

That night, I heard a loud noise from across the house. Emma didn't hear it because she was in the shower. I went to see what the noise was, but there was nothing there. The only thing I saw was that the door was cracked open. I wasn't sure if we had closed it when we came in or left it open due to the hot weather. I shut the door and finished getting ready for bed.

The next morning, I woke up to a noise coming from the guest bedroom. As I ran to the bedroom, I felt my blood run cold. My legs carried me faster than I ever thought they could. When I got to the room, there was nothing in there, but there was a vase that had been knocked over from the bedside table. The window was also open. The window couldn't have been opened by an animal, but I tried to convince myself that Emma had opened it and that a raccoon or some other small animal had come in and tipped over the vase.

As the day went on, I started to notice food wrappers in the house. I just brushed it off, thinking maybe they had been there before and we just hadn't noticed. All of these things become more difficult to shrug off, but I wasn't ready to go home.

Emma and I decided we wanted to go down to the lake and take a swim for a little bit just to cool off. The water seemed to take all of the cares and worries away. I let myself relax and enjoyed the time I had alone with Emma.

After that swim, I no longer worried that there was something or someone in the house every time I heard a noise. I allowed myself fully to forget about the situation. Emma and I spent the rest of the day playing board games. Everything was normal until that night. After we finished playing games and eating dinner, we started getting ready for bed. I heard more noises. It sounded like someone walking through the house. I thought maybe the house was settling, so I decided not to jump to conclusions. This time, it was easier to shrug it off. When we were lying down, we saw what appeared to be something running past the window. It was windy outside, and there were trees right next to the windows, so we didn't think much of it because the dark can play tricks on the mind.

I wouldn't have been so relaxed if I had known then that it was a person outside.

I woke up the next morning (Wednesday) around 8:30 a.m., and Emma wasn't lying next to me like she usually was. I thought she might be up already, making breakfast. I went into the kitchen, but she wasn't there. I searched the house, but there was no sign of her. I went outside to see if she had already gone down to the lake, but again, she was nowhere to be found.

There wasn't much food left in the kitchen, so I thought maybe she had gone to the store. I tried calling her. No answer. I called her seven times. Every time, it went straight to voicemail. At that point, I felt myself getting increasingly worried. The car was still outside, and we had driven together, so she couldn't have gone anywhere. I waited a little bit to see if she had just gone for a walk. She still hadn't returned home when noon approached. Around 1:45 p.m., I called the police. I was worried something had happened to her. The police told me that I had to wait twenty-four hours to file a missing person's report, but they would keep an eye out, in case they saw her. After I got off the phone with the police, I went outside and looked for her some more. Still, I couldn't find her anywhere. She was gone. I continued to wait to see if she would show up, but the day passed, and she never did.

When I tried calling her again, a notification popped up for the local news report. "Lookout for this man!" it read. I became intrigued and noticed there was an article to go along with it. I started reading the article, and it said a man had escaped from the local prison. This man was sentenced to death. He had been imprisoned for murder, kidnapping, and breaking and entering. It said that he had last been seen around the area that we were in. I felt my breathing stop and my heart drop. It was at that moment that all the things that we were hearing and seeing caught up with me.

I immediately called the police and told them about all the things we had heard and seen in the previous two days, and they came out and searched the premises. They didn't find anything but a trail of footprints. The prints seemed to be left by someone with big boots, but they slowly faded after a few feet.

The police searched the area until it was dark. They ended up not finding anything much more than the shoeprints, so they went back to the station to fill out the paperwork.

I went to bed that night terrified. It was so hard to fall asleep.

When I woke up the next morning, some of Emma's things were gone, things that had been there when I fell asleep.

The police wanted me to come to the station so we could discuss the evidence they had found. We discussed several cases that closely resembled my own. They all consisted of girls in their late teens and early twenties going missing in this area. All the things leading up to their disappearances were the same things that had happened to us.

In all the cases, things had gone missing from their homes, food wrappers had been found everywhere, and windows and doors were discovered open; everything was exactly the same.

The police still hadn't found any of the missing girls. They found only the man. They were unable to find this man's true identity because he had burned his fingers to get rid of his fingerprints. He wouldn't tell the police anything. He had been in prison for a little over a year, but he had never said anything about where he had hidden his victims. It was as if he were mute.

The police called in search parties to look for these girls. I couldn't function knowing that there were missing girls being tormented like this, and that my Emma was one of them. The search parties were out for several days.

It wasn't until Sunday that they had some leads. The police had gotten a call from a woman who said she had seen a man in the woods while out on her morning run. Feeling unsafe in his presence, she ran back, but he chased her. She was able to make it out of the woods and seek help before he caught up to her, and she gave a very detailed description of the man.

It was the same person who had been in prison and was suspected of kidnapping the other women. She took the police back to the woods where she had been, and the search parties came to look through all possible areas of the woods. The hope was that if he tried to escape, he would be blocked off. However, he was never found, but they found a clue about where he might have gone.

There was a key for a specific type of shipping container. There was only one place that had shipping containers for sale, so the police started there. They asked the salesman if he had sold any containers lately, and he explained that he had sold one to a guy about a week and a half to two weeks ago. He gave them the spare key and the location where his company had dropped off the container.

The container was in the woods about a mile and a half away from the lake house. Nothing could have prepared me for the terror that struck me to my core when the container was opened.

As the police opened the container, I saw all the missing girls chained up inside. Each and every one of them, including Emma. As I tried to run into the container, the police stopped me.

The police immediately called for the ambulance crews to get these girls. They were all rushed to the hospital in critical condition. Some of the girls had died before we got there. When we arrived at the hospital, the nurses hooked up IVs for each girl so they could get fluids.

They looked like they had been beaten. Luckily, all of them made a full recovery. Some of them were on the verge of dying. If we had gotten there any later, there would've been even fewer to make it out alive. While at the hospital, I got a call from the police station asking if Emma and I could come in. Since she was getting discharged that day, we decided to go.

I had left the decision about going to Emma, and she had decided we would go up there because she wanted justice for herself and the other girls. She was asked to give a description of the man and the things that were done to the girls while she was there, and boy, did she have a story to tell!

After a couple days of being in the container, she kind of started to fade. She hadn't had anything to eat or drink, so she wasn't in the best condition.

She said she only saw the man at night when he came to the container to sleep, but it was so dark, it was kind of hard to see him. All she could say about him was that he was tall. She said he had long, dark, greasy hair. He was very pale and had big feet, but other than that, she didn't know anything else.

When he would come back at night, he would torment them. I'm not going to say what he did because it would get really bad some nights. The next day, they still had the search crews out looking for this man. They ended up finding him in the next town over that same day.

Someone from the town had seen the posters that the police had posted and had actually seen the man. He looked exactly like he did on the posters – the same outfit and everything. The police came immediately and took him into custody. He tried to run, but he didn't make it very far before he was caught.

The police took him back to the station and put him in a cell in the center of the prison. They ended up putting him on death row. There are rumors going around town that he will be executed in a few months.

If I learned anything from this, it's that if you ever have a bad feeling, go with your gut and do what you think is necessary to stay safe.

12. Barbed Wire
By Mary Ella Blankenship and Anne Gammons

Oh, why did he go on the other side of the tree line? I never meant for this to happen. Luke did not deserve this horror. It all happened at 4-H camp.

As soon as the bus came to a complete stop at 4-H camp, all the kids got off, so excited about the fun-filled week before them. However, little did they know, horror was to come.

I introduced myself to another kid on the bus. "Hi, my name is Ella. What's yours?" No reply.

I got my luggage off the back of the bus and headed to the girls' cabin. I didn't know anybody in my cabin; they were all pretty shy. Our counselor's name was Logan. She told us to go to the Rec

Hall, where we would wait for the camp introduction. We had heard that it was really boring, but she still made us go.

In the Rec Hall, we were informed that we would be assigned a color group – green, yellow, red, or blue – for the week. I was assigned the red group. We were also given a schedule for our color group. Then, I met two boys. They seemed pretty nice. I went up to them and asked, "What about this schedule?"

The taller, skinny one whose name was Bryson said, "I know, right? I won't be able to keep up."

Then, Luke, the shorter boy, answered, "Would you like to sit with us?"

"Sure," I replied.

Then, Luke asked, "I wonder what the 'POW' on the old road sign means?"

"It sounds interesting," I told him. "It must relate to the 'Herman the German' story."

"Who's that?" Bryson asked.

I told him, "Herman the German was a World War 2 prisoner here. His ghost roams around the camp at night, looking for the leg he lost while trying to escape years ago. He was shot by a soldier who was guarding the fence. Now, he tries to abduct children to replace his missing limb."

"Oh," Bryson and Luke said.

Luke exclaimed, "That sounds cool! I want to investigate that!"

Later that night, during the campfire, Luke planned to sneak off into the woods. Suddenly, he started to scream, "GUYS, GUESS WHAT! I figured out a plan to find out what is in that creepy, old shed at the top of the hill above the camp! I saw it on the way here and want to explore it!"

Before I continue, I must say that Luke is a very determined person who always tries to find a way to do what he wants. But, anyway, back to the story. Bryson said, "What?"

"I HAVE A PLAN FOR WEDNESDAY NIGHT WHILE EVERYONE IS AT THE CAMPFIRE NIGHT!" screamed Luke. When I tell you everybody in the whole camp was looking at him, they were looking at *him*.

As Rob, the boys' counselor, turned his head, he looked straight at Luke like he was about to suspend him from the camp. Instead, he said, "Mr. Anderson, come up here, please!"

Luke went blank. Even though he was mischievous, he didn't get into trouble much, which was a shocker, and he got good grades. Luke was also a very organized person. But anyway, back to what I was saying.

Rob gave Luke a talking-to, and basically said, "This is your warning. Don't do it again, or you will go home."

So, Luke told us his plan: how he was going to sneak up to the shed, an old POW surgical room on top of the hill, on Wednesday night. He also mentioned that we would come with him.

"Are you crazy, Luke?" whispered Bryson.

"You're going to get us killed!" I said.

I could not stop thinking about Luke's plan as I lay in bed Tuesday night. I thought to myself, "I don't want to go."

On Wednesday morning, I told Luke that I didn't really want to go with him on his adventure.

Then, Bryson said, "If you aren't going, then I'm not either. Sorry, Luke, but you're on your own."

Luke was fine with that, saying he didn't care. He was excited about the night. During the campfire, he was going to go to the bathroom. That was just an excuse to sneak away to the surgical room above the camp, where he was going to explore. Then, if he wasn't back when we returned to the cabins, Bryson was going to cover for him. Bryson and I were very nervous. After all, Luke was our friend.

It was time for the campers to run to the campfire for the best night ever. Tonight, the counselors would tell the famous 'Herman the German' story. It was the best! The campers would eat so much sugar that they would have a hard time getting to sleep that night. When we all sat down around the fire, the counselor said, "Y'all ready to have the best night of your life?"

"YEAH!" everyone yelled.

Luke was ready to sneak off to the hospital room. The campfire started, and I went up and roasted a marshmallow. When I sat back down, I wished Luke good luck. He said, "Thank you," and then asked Rob, his counselor, if he could be excused to go to the bathroom.

That night, everything was weird. I could feel it in the air. After two hours, Luke was still not back, so Bryson covered for him by stuffing clothes and pillows under his covers. Finally, I went to sleep after tossing and turning for many restless hours.

When I woke up, everything seemed like a dream. I got out of bed and went out into the fog, walking to breakfast in the cafeteria. When I arrived, I saw Bryson and went over to him. I asked him where Luke was, and he asked me the same question. I said, "WHAT DO YOU MEAN, 'WHERE IS LUKE?' He came back, right?"

"No," Bryson exclaimed,. "he didn't."

At that moment I knew something was terribly wrong.

"We have to tell somebody," Bryson said.

I told him we needed to wait because if he had come back that morning while we were getting ready for breakfast, he could be in the camp. If that was the case, then Luke would get in trouble with the counselors. He had already gotten in trouble once. Bryson agreed, so our mission now was to find Luke. Unfortunately, we had no luck. So Bryson and I told Rob, the boys' counselor, about Luke's plan to go to the shed upon the hill.

Later that evening, there was still no sign of Luke. Supper was quiet and eerie without him. Every now and then, I would hear the counselors ask each other if anyone heard about Luke's disappearance. They all said, "No," which weakened my hope of finding him. As the night went on, we went to our cabins to get ready for bed. When the lights went out in our cabin, I thought about how we would go home tomorrow, and whether or not we would ever find Luke. Finally, after restless hours, I went to sleep.

Then, I heard the weirdest noise ever. It woke me up so suddenly that I thought it was a dream. I looked outside and saw

Herman the German with Luke's dead, limp body in his arms and one leg cut off, leaving a blood trail from the woods. I looked Herman the German up and down, wondering if this was a dream. Then I noticed something weirdly disturbing: Herman the German had two legs. When I looked closer, I saw that Luke's leg had been sewn in place of his amputated leg. So many questions ran through my head. Was I imagining things? Was this really Luke, or some other kid? I didn't know what to think. I watched as the figure walked toward the woods, staggering with each step. I didn't know what to do. I felt completely useless. I had just figured out what had happened to Luke, but now I couldn't do anything about it. For the rest of the night, I lay in my bed, frozen to the mattress. I did not sleep at all.

When the morning light began to shine through the windows, I slowly climbed out of bed, packed my things, and got ready to load the bus. At breakfast, I didn't mention what I had seen the night before. The image of Luke's cold, limp body in Herman's arms still haunted my mind. After breakfast, everybody loaded onto the bus. I sat and thought about how nobody else would ever know what had happened.

Back home now, many months later, I still feel like I am being followed. At night, I can hear the sound of Herman dragging the sewn-on leg, hunting me because I am the one who saw him that night at 4-H camp.